Margaret Yorke lives in Buckinghamshire. She is a past chairman of the Crime Writers' Association, whose Golden Handcuffs award she received in 1993 in recognition of her contribution to crime writing over many years. In 1982 she won the Swedish Academy of Detection Award for the best crime novel in translation.

The Small Hours of the Morning

MARGARET YORKE

WARNER BOOKS

A *Warner* Book

First published in Great Britain in 1975 by Geoffrey Bles
First published in the United States in 1975
by Walker Publishing Company, Inc.
Published by Penguin Books in 1988

Published by Warner Futura in 1995
Reprinted 1996
Reprinted by Warner Books in 1997, 1998

A CIP catalogue record for this book
is available from the British Library.

ISBN 0 7515 1191 9

Printed in England by Clays Ltd, St Ives plc

Warner Books
A Division of
Little, Brown and Company (UK)
Brettenham House
Lancaster Place
London WC2E 7EN

The
Small Hours
of the Morning

Chapter 1

Cecil Titmuss was a careful man. Whenever he left his car, however briefly, he secured the steering column with a locking device; at night, he emptied the coins from his pockets and sorted them into columns marshalled in an orderly row on his dressing-chest, putting one tenpence piece into a money-box shaped like a hen on a nest and labelled Sedgebay in Gothic script. He recorded daily on a graph the maximum and minimum temperatures as registered beside the back door of The Lindens; a mortice lock was fitted to the front door of the house, and there were bolts on all the windows; he did six press-ups every morning before breakfast and never ate butter. He was a successful practitioner of family planning, the father of a girl aged eight and a boy aged six, now asleep in bed.

June watched him brush his thinning brown hair, trimmed fortnightly, before he joined her in their Slumbersoft divan. He would wind the clock which lived on the shelf by his side of the bed, sigh, kiss her tenderly but without passion, and then fall tidily asleep. Passion was for weekends, and this was Monday.

Tonight, everything happened as she expected. She listened to his even breathing. Cecil did not snore. A chink of light from the street lamp on the corner filtered through the gap in the curtains and cast shadows on the ceiling. A scooter zoomed past, sounding like a monster wasp, but Cecil slept on: a man with a clear conscience, his finances prudently budgeted, his children healthy, his house in order, but his wife at explosion point.

She slipped out of bed, and in only her nightdress went down to the kitchen, where she put on the kettle and lit a cigarette. While the water boiled she stared at her pale reflection in the window pane; it was late summer, and the blind had not been drawn before they went to bed. In the morning the kitchen would smell of tobacco, and Cecil would frown, switch on the extractor fan, but make no other comment.

The kettle boiled. June turned the gas out and abandoned it; instead, she went into the dining-room where there was a half bottle of gin in the sideboard. She poured some out, topped it up with Martini Rosso, and stood by the window drinking it. A comforting warmth began to fill her body, and she filled the glass again, glancing between sips at a piece of paper on the top of the sideboard. It was a competition form. You had to save wrappers from soup tins, place the merits of the soup in order of importance, and compose a slogan; a holiday in the West Indies was the first prize. June often entered such contests, but the thought of Barbados with Cecil did not excite her. She would rather go with the milkman, who had long curling sideburns, enormous blue eyes, and often forgot the yoghurt; he, at least, looked at her as if he admired her.

June could hardly remember the time when Cecil's dependability had been his chief attraction: that was after Barry, to whom she was engaged, had sensationally eloped with the wife of the Baptist minister, five years older than he. If you could call it elope. At any rate, they were married now and had been for years. It still hurt when she thought of it. The minister had retrieved his pride by going on a mission to Uganda; she had fled to Cecil, newly come as branch librarian to Snettlesham and encountered when she handed in, long overdue, *My Family and Other Animals*. She and Barry had planned a honeymoon in Corfu; instead, he went there with the minister's wife

Cecil had fined her, apologetically, for the overdue book, and when he found her still wandering among the shelves unable to choose a replacement, at closing time, had proffered *The Overloaded Ark*. He came out of the building five minutes later and saw her standing on the step looking despairingly at the rain which had begun to fall while she was in the library.

Cecil had an umbrella, although when he left his digs that morning the sun had been shining; it paid to take care and here was his reward. He began by offering to escort her to the bus stop but ended by taking her out to dinner. Three months later they were married. It was the first impulsive action of Cecil's adult life; he had never behaved impetuously again.

June finished her second gin, put the bottles away and wiped a damp mark made by one of them with the hem of her nightdress; then she returned to the kitchen to rinse the glass. On the way upstairs she stubbed her toe and swore softly.

Cecil was still sleeping. He stirred slightly as she slid into bed beside him and one arm moved out to encircle her. It was meaningless, she thought crossly, removing it. She lay with her back to him and closed her eyes. The gin had done the trick and she felt pleasantly swimmy. She thought about palm trees, blue skies and the sea, and tried to imagine the milkman without his white coat and his cap. Before she succeeded she fell asleep.

The watcher across the way saw the lights go out at The Lindens. The scene in the dining-room with June in her nightdress had been clearly visible, each detail magnified because it was observed through binoculars. The unseen witness waited in the surrounding darkness but no other light came on. After some time, on rubber-soled feet, the watcher crept away. It was one o'clock in the morning.

*

Ted Jessop polished the big old Humber lovingly, like a groom rubbing down his favourite horse. He even hissed a little, under his breath. The black bodywork gleamed like jet, and the chrome shone. Not a speck of dust or fluff marred the upholstery inside, nor the deep brown carpeting in the rear. He'd replaced that recently with close-piled tufted; these little things counted. Since he'd helped out Burton, the undertaker, when one of his cars was off the road because of a smash, luckily when returning empty after a funeral, his work had increased. Burton had engaged him for several funerals where extra cars for mourners were needed; he'd followed the sober fleet in and out of the crematorium wearing a solemn expression on his face and a narrow black tie. One thing had led to another; he was booked for weddings most Saturdays now, and because he was dependable he had won some taxi work away from the two firms that operated in Felsbury. Every Tuesday morning he took an old lady into town to shop and change her library book; sometimes she kept him all day while she went to the cinema. He saw the film too, sitting at the back and nipping out before the end so that he was round at the front waiting with the car when she tottered out. He'd met her at one of the funerals. She was a nice old girl; Mrs Malmesbury, her name was, and she lived in one of the new flats at the edge of town. He had to collect her today at eleven o'clock. It cost her a packet to hire him for hours, as she did; but it was cheaper than running a car of her own, which she must have done once. It was a gamble, starting up in the car business. He'd had the chance to buy the Humber cheap, when it had come into Charlie Cooper's workshop almost a write-off. Ted had been working with Charlie ever since he came out of the army. One thing he'd learned during those years was all about engines – and he'd seen the world: the Far East, Cyprus and Germany. He'd saved a bit, and working at nights he'd gradually put the Humber together. He still helped Charlie with repairs when he had time to spare; a skilled mechanic was always in demand. There were occasional lean spells, but they were growing fewer all the time; he'd no wages to pay, and few expenses apart from the car: just his food and the rent. He'd been lucky there, getting a room over a lock-up where the lease had almost run out so that it was cheap; that part of the town was due for re-development and by the time the council got round to pulling it all down he should have enough for something more permanent, even if it had to be out of town. If he'd built up a clientele by then, moving from the centre wouldn't matter.

It was dull work, sometimes, with the old ladies and the funerals; but weddings were livelier, and so were trips to the airport. There were tourists, too, and that paid well; Americans expected a large, comfortable car and a driver who knew his way around. Ted enjoyed those days out. There were often sizeable tips as well as the fare; they didn't realize that he was the gaffer.

Mrs Malmesbury would emerge punctually from the block of flats, and he'd hand her into the car as if she were precious cargo. After all, she had been precious once, to Mr Malmesbury, presumably, who must have left her well provided for. There weren't any children; she'd told him that her only son, a fighter pilot, had been killed in the war.

Today she had to go to the dentist before they went to the library. Ted drew up outside Mr Bryan Vigors' surgery and helped Mrs Malmesbury out of the car on to the pavement. He rang the bell and waited with her till the door was opened. An unsmiling young woman with a sallow complexion and dark hair coiled round her head, wearing a neat white coat, opened it and stood back. Mrs Malmesbury, awkwardly because of her arthritic hip, mounted the step and crossed the threshold. Ted, about to assure her that he would be right outside when she emerged, found the door closed firmly in his face. He stood staring at the purple gloss paint for a moment, his jaw half-open, as the phrase died still-born.

'Stuck up bitch,' he said aloud, instead, referring to the girl, and went back to the car. One advantage of Mr Vigors' surgery was that it was on the outskirts of the town and parking was allowed. Mrs Malmesbury had said she would not be long; Mr Vigors rarely kept her waiting, it appeared. Trouble with her dentures, Ted supposed. He debated popping up the road for a coffee, but decided against it; the old girl might be quicker than she expected, and it would never do if she came out to find him gone. He took a paperback book out of the glove compartment and settled down behind the wheel. He'd always enjoyed a bit of a read, and there was a lot of waiting about on this job; you couldn't polish Bess, as he called his car after the highwayman's steed, for ever.

'Good morning, Mrs Malmesbury. How are you?' boomed Mr Bryan Vigors as Mrs Malmesbury came panting into his surgery. The steep climb up the stairs was a great effort for her, with her painful hip, and that girl had shot up ahead, impatience manifest in every thrust of her skinny legs.

Mr Vigors helped her into the chair and murmured about the weather while Mrs Malmesbury got her breath back.

'A little pain,' she told him, and indicated a molar.

'Yes, hm.' Mr Vigors bent over her and his large brown eyes gazed into her mouth. He was a big man with a curling auburn beard which he hid under a surgical mask while working. He surveyed Mrs Malmesbury's teeth: she had three on a small plate, and the rest were her own, with a gap or two; not bad for her age. 'It ought to come out,' he said, and frowned. He would not like her to travel home by bus after an extraction at her age.

'Did you come on the bus?' he asked.

'No. In a hired car.' Mrs Malmesbury explained about Ted. 'He takes me out shopping once a week. He's such a nice young man, and so reliable.'

'And he's picking you up later?'

'He's waiting outside,' said Mrs Malmesbury.

'Ah, good. We'll do it now, then. You won't miss this one,' said Mr Vigors. It shouldn't upset her, but you could never be certain. She was a frail old thing, getting on for eighty.

'Miss Gibson.' He spoke to the nurse, and asked her to prepare the injection.

Mrs Malmesbury bore the needle with fortitude. At her age there was constant need for endurance every day, but she had learned, while cultivating stoicism, to find compensating pleasure in small things: in the genuine concern, for instance, of Mr Vigors, intent on making the extraction as easy as possible. She looked fleetingly away from his tray of equipment to the dark young woman standing by the chair, but there was no comfort in her expressionless eyes.

While the injection took effect Mr Vigors scraped and scaled away at the other teeth. The old lady seemed as fragile as a bird; her little bones would crush as easily. Gently his sensitive fingers worked round her mouth. Miss Gibson retreated and filled in the chart. She was efficient; he wished he liked her better, thought Mr Vigors as she appeared with a kidney bowl to accept the extracted tooth.

'I didn't feel it at all,' said Mrs Malmesbury, with truth. She trembled a little however, and spat bloodily into the basin. Mr Vigors did not hurry. That was one thing about private practice; you could take time.

'All right, then?' He helped her from the chair. 'Would you like to rest a little, in the waiting-room?'

Lorna Gibson made as if to take Mrs Malmesbury's arm and then drew back. The old lady gathered herself together.

'No, no. I'm quite all right, thank you, Mr Vigors,' she said. 'Goodbye.'

She hobbled painfully down the stairs. What a pity Mr Vigors' surgery was not on the ground floor. A chiropodist worked there. Perhaps people with bad feet were less able to climb stairs than those with dental trouble, she reflected, plodding downwards. The girl, Miss Gibson, preceded her and stood waiting in the hall, her hand hovering ready to open the door.

Mr Vigors, on the landing, saw that Lorna made no attempt to help the old lady negotiate the awkward turn half-way down the stairs; in a few bounds he descended, took Mrs Malmesbury by the elbow, and almost lifted her the rest of the way, giving Lorna a baleful look as he did so.

'There. All right?' He personally handed her out of the door.

Ted was ready; Mrs Malmesbury was stowed inside the car and driven away.

'I'm sorry, Mr Vigors,' Lorna forestalled the rebuke. 'I should have helped her down. I just couldn't touch her.'

'Not touch her?' Vigors barked the words. 'Why ever not?'

'I don't know. I can't explain,' said Lorna. 'The next patient's waiting.'

She went ahead of him up the stairs and was soon busy putting the surgery straight and laying out fresh implements.

Not touch her? Mrs Malmesbury didn't smell. She was a particularly nice old lady, in Mr Vigors' opinion.

The thought formed that, despite her efficiency, Lorna might have to go: she lacked some vital quality, but what was it?

*

14

'That poor old thing. Why couldn't I do it?' Lorna asked herself as she ate her lunch in the office where she and Nancy, the other girl who worked for Mr Vigors, did the accounts, kept the records and made tea. Nancy was away this week, on holiday with Joe, her merchant seaman boyfriend; she did most of the chairside work and Lorna the clerical, but Mr Vigors insisted that each should sometimes double for the other. Nancy had been with him for three years; she was a cheerful girl who mothered the patients when it was necessary. She was not disturbed by Lorna's moodiness; her efficiency more than compensated for it. Lorna's predecessor had been livelier, but scatter-brained.

Lorna's lunch was two cheese sandwiches and an apple. She made some tea, and while she drank it gazed out of the window at the garden below. Mr Vigors' patch was small: a square of lawn bordered with shrubs. The chiropodist, an elderly man who would soon be retiring, used it at lunch-time, and so did Nancy; but Lorna seldom joined them, though she wanted to. She longed for the ability to sit chatting casually, as they did, but paralysing shyness made her brusque and awkward whenever she tried, and she imagined the atmosphere grew hostile to her, so she kept away. She and Nancy opened the front door to Mr Carruthers' patients but did no other work for him. A part-time secretary sorted out his papers.

Under Lorna's sole rule the office was neat; when Nancy was there she left bag, make-up, scarf and oddments all over the place, but Lorna was tidy. She perched on the window-sill and watched Mr Carruthers, below in a deck-chair, reading the *Daily Express*. Mr Vigors either went home to his beautiful wife or to The Grapes on the corner, though he never drank at midday for it would not do to breathe fumes over his two o'clock patient.

There was washing on the line in the garden next door:

a child's dress, small shorts and a shirt. A young woman came and unpegged them as Lorna watched, then went indoors again. All the warmth of family life was in there, Lorna thought; little bodies, soft and round to hug, and a man coming home. Her imagination dwelt on it, part fascinated, part frightened. What must such a life be like?

'Why am I like this?' she wondered. 'Why am I afraid?'

And Bryan Vigors, embracing his wife before reluctantly leaving her to return to the surgery, echoed her thought.

'That girl who's so good at the paperwork – Lorna Gibson. She's a very odd creature,' he said. 'Hates touching people.'

'Well, she's right to be choosy,' said Susan, smoothing his beard.

'What about old ladies?' said Bryan, and described what had happened.

'How very peculiar,' said Susan. 'Repressed, I suppose, but I thought no one was, nowadays.' She gently tweaked the auburn hairs. 'Poor Lorna Gibson.'

A new town centre and shopping precinct had been built in Felsbury as part of its re-development programme, and a fine modern library occupied one corner of a concrete block which also contained the civic offices. It was a large library with an extensive reference section and a stack in the basement of works only occasionally required. Cecil Titmuss was the deputy librarian, and every time he entered the bright new premises he felt a thrill. This was a very different place from the branch library in Snettlesham, which was cramped and drab, with chocolate-brown paint on the woodwork and beige walls wherever there were no shelves. It was a hallowed place, though, for he had met June there. They had moved to Felsbury just before house prices went wild and had bought a Victorian villa in

16

a quiet suburb. Cecil had been promoted to his present post a year ago.

One of the disadvantages of his new position was that much of the work was administrative. He no longer spent much time among the books and readers but passed his working hours writing reports and dealing with policy. He did all this in an office separated from the public part of the library by glass partitions shielded from the readers' gaze by venetian blinds kept in the open-slat position. Cecil looked through them at intervals to see what was going on beyond, in the lending library. He knew many patrons not only by sight but by name. Several old men spent hours there every week, reading the papers and snoozing in the comfort of the council's rexine-covered seats. There were students who worked in the reference section, and there was Peter Guthrie, a local author, who came in frequently. He would collect a dozen or so books at a time to read up some campaign or battle for the four novels he turned out every year under two different names. Under his own he had begun, after the war, writing a series of novels forming a saga set in the time of Marlborough, and featuring a recurring hero who rose gradually from cornet to colonel throughout the sequence, meanwhile breaking the hearts of various females with names like Clarissa and Emmeline. In his other *persona*, as Tom Fowler, he wrote about a private eye perpetually saving his country from disaster threatened by an unnamed foreign power which employed ingenious schemes ranging from germ warfare to mass hypnosis.

Guthrie was in the library now. Cecil could see him talking to Miss Binks at the desk; he was beaming at her genially: telling her about his new book, no doubt. One had appeared the week before, wherein his hero nipped in the bud an attempt to contaminate the nation's water supply with a drug which would sap everyone's moral fibre and cause unlicensed conduct to run rampant.

17

'It does already,' said the head librarian dourly, reading the blurb soon after the police had rounded up twenty young people alleged to be having an orgy.

Cecil went through the glass dividing doors and into the library, where he intercepted Guthrie as he left the desk.

'Good morning, Mr Guthrie. How's *Saturnalia at Seven* doing?' he asked.

'Oh – mustn't complain,' said the author, waving his pipe. He was a large man, broadly built, his rubicund face framed with modish sideburns and with iron-grey hair falling about his neck in trendy abundance. 'There's a Guthrie due before Christmas – Gadsby's a general now.'

'No, really?' Gadsby was the Malplaquet hero. 'Well!' Cecil could find no more to say, but it was enough. Guthrie boomed on about the book; his voice was loud and resonant, and people turned to look at him. To his credit he seemed unaware of the attention he attracted; his books were very popular; they gave pleasure and fulfilled a need. Foreign sales and paperback rights ensured a comfortable income for the author.

A small commotion behind the two men interrupted their amiable exchange. An elderly lady who was approaching the desk gave a moan and folded neatly into a bundle, collapsing on to the polished lino.

'Dear me, dear me,' said Guthrie, stooping down and raising Mrs Malmesbury's head – for it was she – on one Harris-tweed arm.

'Put her head back. Raise her feet,' commanded Cecil in a voice of authority. He had done a first-aid course; you never knew what might happen in a library. This was not the first time he'd been thankful for his own foresight. 'She'll soon come round.'

But she didn't. They kept the other readers away from her prostrate form, but one woman, who said she was a nurse, joined them, bending over the limp figure. After a whispered conference Guthrie handed his pipe to Cecil to

18

carry, bent down, and picked up Mrs Malmesbury. She was so small and thin that she was no heavier than a child, and it was no effort for the big man to carry her out of the library into an office. Here they spread her across three large chairs pushed together to form a sort of couch.

'She may have had a heart attack. She's very cyanosed,' said the nurse. 'We'd better call an ambulance.'

Mrs Malmesbury went to the library every week, and while she did so Ted always drove away, returning after twenty minutes. A car with a uniformed driver could halt briefly on the double yellow line outside the library; if challenged by a warden he merely said he was waiting for an elderly invalid and was never forced to move. Today, he had been waiting for some time and was beginning to wonder what was delaying Mrs Malmesbury when an ambulance arrived, siren sounding and light flashing. Soon, a little procession came down the steps from the library: the stretcher, the off-duty nurse, Titmuss, and the tall figure of Peter Guthrie.

Ted knew immediately who was on the stretcher.

'Whatever's happened?' He stepped forward. 'Not dead, is she?' He looked down. Very little of Mrs Malmesbury could be seen above the grey blanket.

'You know her?' Cecil asked.

'I'm her driver.'

'Best come on to the hospital, mate, and give her particulars,' said one of the ambulance men.

'Yes. All right. I'd better, I suppose,' said Ted. Poor old girl. He hadn't liked the look of her when she came out of the dentist's, and had suggested taking her straight home. She'd agreed to cut the rest of the day short but insisted on changing her books; she'd nothing to read and they were keeping something for her, she explained. Then she'd refused to let Ted go up and change them for her.

'The exercise will do me good,' she'd said.

'I'll come along too,' said Guthrie. He'd nothing to do

before lunch, which he was having in town, and it would fill in the time. Besides, it might provide copy: you never knew what would prove a useful experience.

'All right,' agreed Ted. Why not? The fellow had been there when Mrs Malmesbury was taken ill, it seemed. He could be a help.

'That's very good of you, Mr Guthrie,' said Cecil, thus absolved from further responsibility.

The little group broke up, and Cecil returned to the library.

'She never took her book,' said Miss Binks, holding a biography of Emmeline Pankhurst to her polyester bosom. 'Shall I let the next person on the list have it, Mr Titmuss?'

'No. Don't do that, Miss Binks,' said Cecil. 'If she's to be ill, she'll need something to read. I'll take it round to her.'

'But there isn't a ticket, Mr Titmuss. She'd not given back her other books.'

'That's quite all right. I'll collect them from her,' Cecil said. Mrs Malmesbury's shopping bag had been gathered up with her and put in the ambulance. 'It's my responsibility, Miss Binks,' he added in austere tones, as the girl regarded him disapprovingly.

'Very well, Mr Titmuss,' said Miss Binks.

Cecil went back to his office and made a brief note of the whole incident, the names of those concerned, even that of the off-duty nurse. You could not trust your memory entirely after the passage of time, and details might matter later.

Peter Guthrie enjoyed driving along in the Humber. He and Ted went into the casualty department together and supplied what facts they could about Mrs Malmesbury, who was swiftly wheeled away. She had begun to stir and looked less blue by this time. They had been unable to give the names of any relatives, but Ted volunteered to make enquiries at Cleveland Court, the block of flats where she lived.

'Those are nice flats,' said Guthrie, who lived in a village six miles out of town. 'Drop me back in the town, will you? I've left my car in the municipal park.'

Ted did as he was bid. Guthrie talked to him as they went along and soon learned how he had started up the car-hire business and about his army life. Guthrie had fought in the desert during the war; he was brooding on a new series about a tank commander in the fight against Rommel: war books were all the rage just now. He'd need another pseudonym for that. Ted gave him one of his business cards when they parted: you never knew; he seemed an important sort of character and might have friends needing a car. It wasn't until he put the car away, late that night, and took the paperback book he'd been reading out of the glove compartment that he realized who his passenger was: on the back of the book was Guthrie's photograph.

Chapter 2

The library remained open until eight o'clock five evenings a week, and Cecil took his turn at late duty like everyone else, but on Tuesdays he left at five. By this time Felsbury was starting its rush-hour and the traffic was heavy. Cecil unlocked the steering-wheel, started the car and edged out of his reserved parking space. Library concerns flowed out of his mind and it filled instead with domestic matters as he joined the stream of cars. Tonight June was going to her Italian class, and he would have an undisturbed evening to work on the model of Notre Dame which he was building from matchsticks. The whole plan was graphed out like an architect's design and fixed to the wall in the dining-room, which was used by the family as a general living room. Cecil had calculated the number of matches he would require; most of the elevations were already fixed. He worked by the light of an anglepoise lamp and used stamp tweezers to place the matches in position. He had already built Westminster Abbey, Wells Cathedral and York Minster, and planned to do all the major ecclesiastical buildings in Europe.

June's choice of evening class was affected by which night she could attend, for it had to be one when Cecil finished early, because of the children. She had not felt drawn towards badminton or yoga, also available on Tuesdays; she longed to visit Italy, and thought that if she learned a little of the language Cecil might be persuaded that they should go there instead of to Sedgebay yet again; the children were old enough now, and it needn't be expensive. In any case, June had determined to find the money herself: she had gone back to work, now that both children were at school.

Cecil sighed, thinking of this. June was a trained florist, and she had found a part-time post at Floradora's. He had to admit that so far it had proved a success; nothing suffered at home, and June seemed brighter than for a long time. She worked only in the mornings; in the school holidays she intended to find a play-group for the children, or pay a sixth-form schoolgirl to look after them. Her independence frightened Cecil; he had never, as a young man, imagined that he would marry anyone so spirited, and indeed when he met June most of her natural fire had been quenched by the blow to her pride, if not her heart, delivered by Barry. He had pictured himself with a biddable girl who would look up to him; instead, he'd got a vigorous woman who mocked his cautious ways. She had sudden brief crazes for projects like making lamp-shades, which she sold to a Felsbury store; they at least paid for themselves, unlike the guitar lessons she tried for a time. Her surplus energy was better channelled into regular hours at Floradora's, he supposed; perhaps she would now give up those silly competitions, which fascinated her; he was heartily tired of the breakfast cereal they had been forced to eat for weeks while she collected enough vouchers to compete for a redesigned kitchen; now it was Simpson's soups, when home-made broth was much more nutritious.

Cecil felt guilty about enjoying his solitude on June's evenings out; there was no challenge to him, when she was not there; he could relax. But he was not entirely free from anxiety when she took the car; he knew she never bothered to immobilize it properly; she was careless, too, and bad at parking, likely to scrape a wing or dent a bumper, though her road sense was good.

He was home in time to read to the children before they

went to bed; he did this every evening except when he worked late, when it was June's task. He suspected that she did not always do it, for he would find the children clamouring to continue from the place where he had last left the story, though their loyal excuse was always that he must not miss any part of the tale.

Tonight they read another chapter of *The Wind in the Willows* while June got ready to go out. Cecil read extremely well, adopting different tones for each animal in the story, and the children were spellbound, Janet, in her red woollen dressing-gown, cuddling up against him as they sat together on Barty's bed, while the little boy stared solemnly at his father.

June came to say goodnight before she left. She paused on the landing before entering the room, and listened to the gruff voice of Badger and the bluster of Toad: it was strange that Cecil was so good at this.

He went down to see her off. She wore brown slacks, an orange sweater, and a dark-brown trench coat: she looked wonderful. He watched the car disappear round the corner and then went slowly back into the house; he knew no more about what June thought of things now than when they were married, in fact sometimes he felt that she was becoming more unreal to him all the time. When they made love he marvelled at his own presumption and in the morning he could never believe that it had really happened. But there were the children: no one could dispute that, and with them he was wholly at ease. He did not yet anticipate the years ahead when they might grow rebellious; now they were tractable, and they loved him.

He thought himself a happy and fortunate man.

June stopped on her way to the technical college, where her evening classes were held, to post her completed soup competition entry. There was a branch of the Midland

Bank on the corner a few doors away from the post office, and she noticed a man fumbling at a fixture on the wall outside it; the night safe, she realized. Joyce Watson, her employer at Floradora's, used one to avoid leaving cash in unoccupied premises. As Felsbury expanded fewer people lived in the town centre; the upper floors over shops were mostly offices now. June got back into the car, passed a Hillman Imp parked opposite to the bank, and drove on towards the college.

There was much activity going on when she arrived; men and women in white garments, clutching badminton rackets, sauntered about; some trousered figures went off to their yoga. It was the second week of term, and enthusiasm was still strong in most pupils; June had enjoyed her first Italian lesson; it seemed an easier language than French. By next summer she should have saved enough for them all to go to Venice – the Lido, for the children. Cecil, she was sure, would like to see St. Marks; to build that out of matchsticks would certainly be a challenge.

She went into the classroom and joined her fellow pupils, waiting for their teacher.

Ted Jessop spent a frustrating time at Cleveland Court trying to make some contact for Mrs Malmesbury. There was no porter, so he rang the bells of the flats on either side of hers, but got no answer. In the end he left a note for the janitor. How isolated from one another the inhabitants of the big block must be; he wondered if the hospital would send someone round to fetch the old lady's belongings – she must want a few of her own bits and pieces.

A trip to the airport cropped up that afternoon, and in the evening he had to take two aldermen to a dinner; such engagements often came his way, for the city dignitaries did not care to chance the breathalyser by driving themselves. He delivered them, then went back to the mews and cooked himself sausages and packet potato for his supper. As he ate he kept thinking about Mrs Malmesbury. To set his mind at rest about her, he decided to go early for the aldermen and call in at the hospital on the way. Someone would tell him if the old lady was on the mend or not, and whether they'd found any relative.

She was improving, he learned. No one had brought round her nightdress, but she didn't need it; she was in a hospital gown. She was well enough now to tell Sister or the social worker whom to get in touch with; there was a friend who lived nearby, it seemed. Ted remembered that sometimes Mrs Malmesbury met another elderly lady for lunch.

Slightly reassured, Ted left. He had time in hand, so he drove down the road intending to drop in at a pub for a quick half pint before he collected his fares – that would not jeopardize his driving ability. He parked in a quiet street near The Crown; it was close to the technical college, and as he went by the students were coming out after their evening classes. Ted had a friend who taught motor maintenance there, though on which night of the week, Ted did not know. He walked slowly towards the building with the idea of seeing if Jack would join him at the pub. The forecourt in front of the college was full of cars and there was much to-ing and fro-ing as they manoeuvred to leave. Dusk was falling, and the late September air smelled autumnal. A face he recognised caught Ted's attention as a tall, angular girl came out of the gate, wheeling a bicycle. It was that stuck-up bitch from the dentist's place.

He'd tell her about poor old Mrs Malmesbury. Maybe the dentist gave her the wrong dope. Ted turned after her.

'Hey – excuse me!' he called, but Lorna took no notice.

Too high and mighty by half, thought Ted, not

realizing that his intentions might be misconstrued. He stepped in front of her, and she stared at him blankly. As if I smelled or something, he thought.

'Excuse me. You work for Mr Vigors, don't you?' he said.

'Yes.' Lorna had not recognized him at first, but as he explained, she remembered him. He wore no uniform cap now, but was still dressed in his navy-blue suit.

He described what had happened at the library.

'Oh – I'm sorry. It couldn't have been the treatment,' said Lorna, swift to defend her employer.

'Maybe not. But I thought I'd tell you, all the same,' said Ted. The girl looked less toffee-nosed now; her eyes had flickered with something like alarm when he spoke to her.

'I'll tell Mr Vigors,' she said.

'Right, then,' said Ted. He was about to move away when something made him glance at her again; she looked frightened. 'Going to evening classes, then, are you?' he asked, in a more friendly voice.

'Yes,' said Lorna, and since he still stood there blocking her path, added, 'Italian.'

'Oh yes? That's nice.'

'Yes.'

Ted could think of no more to say. She stood there woodenly, and the blank look returned to her face.

'Goodnight, then,' said Ted, moving out of her way.

'Goodnight,' Lorna answered, and pedalled off.

Ted turned back towards the college. He might have missed Jack by now, assuming he'd been there at all, but cars were still coming through the gates. Above the sound of revving engines came the whirr-whirr of a starter that would not engage.

It was a cream Morris 1300, old, but well cared for, and the driver was a young woman with a cloud of thick chestnut-brown hair which now fell across her face as she impotently twisted the key.

'You'll run your battery down. Let's have a look,' said Ted, approaching. 'Got petrol, have you?'

'What? Yes – tank's full,' said June Titmuss. 'I don't know what can be wrong. It was perfectly all right coming over.'

Ted opened the bonnet, lifted a lead from one of the plugs, and held it against the plug body.

'Try it again,' he said.

June obeyed, with the same result.

'Ah! Thought so! No spark,' said Ted. He took the cap off the distributor. 'Points. Usually is, when there's no spark. Won't take a tick.'

He took a handkerchief out of his pocket and bent over the engine. June got out of the car and came to watch the operation. Her rescuer had large, square hands with stubby fingers which moved dextrously; the dirty points were soon wiped clean.

'There, that should do it,' he said.

'Was that all it needed?' June asked, amazed.

'I've just given them a wipe for now, but they'll want proper cleaning soon, or it'll happen again,' he said. 'Try her,' he added, and looked at June properly for the first time.

She had huge eyes of an unusual brown colour, warmer than most brown eyes; he could discern this much in spite of the indifferent lighting outside the college. A faint fragrance came from her, and she was just the right height. All this he noticed as she got back into the car.

It started at once.

'Can I give you a lift?' she asked.

'No – no thanks. I've got my car,' said Ted.

'See you next week, then,' said June. 'And thanks very much.'

She must think he was another student. Well, where was the harm in that?

'Yes,' he agreed. 'Next week.'

He watched her depart. The car jerked as she moved forward, letting the clutch in roughly, something that ordinarily would have annoyed him; he could not bear to see machinery maltreated. But this girl with the warm brown eyes must be forgiven; she probably didn't get enough practice, he thought tolerantly as she set off. A hand came out of the window and waved to him.

'Thanks again,' she called.

There was no reason at all why he should not see her next week.

The driver of the Hillman Imp which June had passed on her way to the college watched an elderly man deposit a bag in the night safe at the Midland Bank and then walk off. Ray Brett got out of the car and followed on foot; they went half a mile up the road, turned left down another, and then his quarry stopped at a bus-stop. Ray sighed. Another dead end unless he could whip back in the car before the bus arrived. He loped away; the bus was disappearing round a distant bend when he drove back. Ray fell in behind.

The man he had followed got off in a residential street on the edge of the town. Ray drove past him, parked, and in the mirror watched him turn in at the gate of a grey pebble-dashed semi-detached house. He drove on, turned, and on the way back noted the number. Then he returned to the corner opposite the bank. He stayed there for an hour but no one else used the night safe while he was watching.

There had been a number of callers at the bank that evening, and he'd followed them all. Only one had gone back to commercial premises: Floradora, in the person of a plump middle-aged woman with bright blonde hair, had returned to a florist's near the town hall. Everyone else had gone off in cars or caught buses. He'd followed some of them. In order to trace where they came from before going to the bank, and thus see if they were likely to be dropping substantial sums into the safe, he'd have to pick them up in reverse order in the morning and follow them from their homes to their work.

He reckoned he'd get away with maybe three jobs. Then he'd have to move on and work the same game somewhere else. So he needed to be sure of three worthwhile hauls; a few hundred quid each time, at the least. With that behind him he could leave Felsbury and go north, or to London; then he'd try to get in with a mob of some sort. That was the way to the really big stuff. So far he'd been a lone operator; he'd nearly got nicked once, breaking and entering, and the results weren't all that great. But this was a good idea; if he pulled it off he'd have something to boast of when he tried to get in with an established gang, and money to flash around.

Ray lived in a council flat with his parents and two younger brothers. His mother worked two afternoons at the laundry, and several mornings at cleaning jobs; his father was employed at a canning factory. They were respectable people who did not know that their eldest child was amoral.

When Ray came into the flat later that night his mother was mending a torn shirt that belonged to his next brother.

'Where've you been, then, Ray?' she asked, looking up at him over the spectacles she wore for close work.

'Oh, down the club,' said Ray. He was a token member of a youth club. It kept them quiet at home, and he went there when he'd nothing better to do.

The television was on and his father was watching a boxing match. Ray picked up the *Daily Mirror*. Like his parents, he had a respectable job; he drove a grocer's delivery van.

*

The watcher could see Cecil in the dining-room; the lamps were on now but the curtains were not drawn. He was seated at the table working at some sort of model-making; a skeleton structure was visible but it was impossible to make out the details. A small bald circle showed on the crown of his head; his shoulders were bowed as he bent over his work. After a while he looked at his watch, got up and went out of the room, then returned and resumed his task. Soon there was the sound of a car stopping, and of doors shutting; more lights came on in the house, one upstairs in the main bedroom. June Titmuss was visible briefly, before she drew the curtains. Then the upstairs light went out, and Cecil appeared below, this time carrying a tray laden with teapot and cups. June came in, said something, and gestured. Cecil set down the tray, crossed to the window and drew the curtains.

The watcher stayed for a long time, waiting until first the lights downstairs went out and then, much later, those upstairs were finally extinguished.

June did not tell Cecil about the car's failure; she was tempted to, because he took such care of it, recording its servicing particulars meticulously and watching its oil consumption like an anxious mother weighing the milk intake of her infant, and to prove his system fallible would have given her immense satisfaction. Besides, her rescuer had said it might go wrong again. But she wanted to keep the incident to herself because their meeting had disturbed her; she kept seeing him again as he bent over the car, the thick, springy hair curling round his ears. What was his name, she wondered. Well, she would find out when they met next week.

She did not go back to the gin bottle. With her job to occupy the mornings, her day was full; it was quite a rush to get through the cleaning and shopping and be at the school in time to collect the children every afternoon. The Lindens was a drab-looking house, built of brownish brick; June got no pleasure from its appearance, and often urged Cecil to think of moving to a new estate, but he would never agree. Their mortgage would increase, if they did this, and they would lose the large garden and all the space in the old house; there were plenty of cupboards and even enough room for Cecil's models. Wells Cathedral and York Minster each had a wide window-ledge to itself on the landing.

She liked working at Floradora's. She had lost none of her skill, and her employer Joyce Watson's only regret was that she could not stay all day. June, in fact, hoped to do so later, when the children were older; meanwhile, the arrangement was that she would help out when there was extra work such as a big funeral or a smart wedding. The children could come to the shop, if necessary, and play quietly at the back while wreaths or bouquets were assembled. Mrs Watson had swiftly assessed June, in fact, as a bored young woman; once she had found some degree of independence she would begin to assert herself; she would soon be staying until it was time to fetch the children from school.

A few days after Mrs Malmesbury's collapse, Cecil admitted to June that perhaps her return to work had been a good idea. She looked brighter for it, more blooming, somehow, as if working among the flowers were in some way therapeutic. He liked quiet places himself, such as libraries, but June was livelier than he; perhaps she needed the constant bustle.

Not that days in the library were uneventful. He told her about Mrs Malmesbury being taken ill. He had been round to the hospital, taking with him the Emmeline Pankhurst book and bringing back her others, to the relief of Miss Binks who still felt she would somehow be called

32

to account for the lack of a borrower's ticket. Mrs Malmesbury did not feel quite up to Emmeline Pankhurst yet, but she was grateful; he saw her for a minute, propped up on pillows and wearing her hospital gown.

It was like him to go round and see the old lady, June thought; he was a kindly man.

When Lorna told Mr Vigors about Mrs Malmesbury's collapse he was shocked.

'Ring up the hospital and find out how she is,' he instructed. He knew he had taken every care with his patient and that his treatment could not be responsible; nevertheless, the extraction might have led to more shock than she showed at the time, and if she were to die it could lead to awkward questions from the coroner. It was a relief to be told that she was improving; he must remember to enquire again in a few days, and asked Lorna to make a note of it.

Just before one o'clock the doorbell rang. No patient was expected until two, and when Lorna opened the door she found Susan Vigors outside.

'Hullo,' she said. 'You're Lorna, I know. Is Bryan still probing away? Tell him I've come, would you? His wife,' she added, as Lorna hesitated, her body athwart the door in a defensive position.

'Is he expecting you?' asked Lorna.

'No. It's a surprise. I'm going to make him give me lunch,' said Susan, and floated past Lorna into the waiting-room which Bryan shared with Mr Carruthers. Her long, dark hair bobbed on her shoulders and a waft of expensive scent came from her; she had an aura of sheer animal vitality which made the other girl shrink from her, repelled.

Lorna trod back up the stairs to where Vigors was drilling the tooth of a local magistrate.

'Mrs Vigors is here,' she said in a flat voice.

Bryan Vigors never took his eyes from his task, but even so, Lorna saw them light up. He stopped the drill.

'One silver,' he said.

Lorna prepared the filling. In silence Vigors stopped the tooth, pressing the metal neatly into place and smoothing it off; then he bade the magistrate remain seated, open-mouthed like a gasping fish, while it hardened.

'Excuse me,' said the dentist, and disappeared. Lorna heard him bounding down the stairs. She began to clear up around the magistrate.

Mr Vigors returned, beaming, made sure the filling was comfortable and pumped the chair down. The magistrate departed, and Vigors went after him, rushing off like an eager schoolboy.

Lorna went on stolidly clearing up the surgery. She heard laughter, unrepressed, floating up from the hallway below. There was no need for her to go downstairs; her lunch was in the office; but she did. From halfway down she saw the Vigors, arms linked, approaching the door; they stopped to embrace and stood entwined, gazing into each other's eyes with undisguised delight and in complete disregard of anyone else. Still laughing, at last they went out, and banged the door behind them.

Tears pricked at Lorna's eyes. They had been married for at least ten years, and had three children, yet their absorption in each other was total.

I'd be different, if that could happen to me, thought Lorna. I can't touch even an old lady, because no one touches me. Not ever.

And it was true. She might bump against someone by chance, in a bus or a crowded shop, drawing away at once; otherwise she had no physical contact of any sort at all. It was a part of life she did not understand.

Chapter 3

On Thursday Ted had to take someone who was not eligible for an ambulance home from the hospital. On the way he remembered Mrs Malmesbury, and seeing a vacant parking space near the town hall, he slid the Humber into it and walked down to Floradora's to buy her some flowers.

There, in the shop, was the girl whose car he had fixed two nights before. They stared at one another for a moment, and then both broke into pleased, bubbling laughter; Cecil would have been surprised if he had heard June laugh like this, and Lorna might have identified it as being akin to the spontaneous merriment shared between Bryan and Susan Vigors.

'Well,' said Ted. 'Hullo, there.'

'Hullo,' said June.

'Car all right?'

'Fine, thanks. No more trouble.'

She was certainly quite something. He'd not been wrong, the other night. Amber eyes, a freckled nose, and gleaming chestnut hair. What a pity he hadn't time to linger now, when she was alone in the shop.

'I want a few flowers for someone ill,' he said. 'Nothing expensive.'

'How about these?' She showed him some small pink chrysanthemums.

'They'll do fine. Sorry I'm in a rush,' he said. 'I'd like to stay and chat.'

'I'm working,' she pointed out, with a mock prim look. 'Do you want to write a card?'

'What? Oh, yes, I'd better, I suppose.'

She gave him one, and an envelope, and wrapped the flowers while he wrote it. She did not look at it as she took the money from him.

'See you on Tuesday?'

'Why not?' said June lightly.

Ted drove off whistling cheerfully. She'd got wide lips and a figure that curved in all the right places, for all she was wearing an overall. What a bit of luck that he'd thought of the flowers: now he knew where she worked, in case he missed her on Tuesday. But he wouldn't. If anyone wanted the car that night, he'd refuse the booking.

Ray had tracked down one of the night-safe depositors to Tansy's Tea Shoppe, near the town hall. It was chance; he'd seen the man on a ladder cleaning the big bow window as he drove by in the grocery van. There'd be a tidy sum in the till of a place like that on a Saturday.

The idea had come to Ray when he'd seen his own employer, Mr Crawley, stuffing his takings into a shabby leather bag ready to drop in the safe himself. But it would be crazy to do old Crawley – much too near home. However, the thought had taken root; it was clever, Ray felt. He'd taken the job at Crawley's because there was nothing else going that he fancied at the time and he thought it would offer scope for knocking off cigarettes and the odd bottle of spirits. But such booty had to be sold; if he could get hold of actual cash he'd be on to the big money in no time. Working it all out was exciting; he thought about it most of the time and was on the lookout, all the while, for likely victims.

Meanwhile, he was a model delivery man. Crawley's was one of the few old-fashioned grocery stores flourishing against supermarket competition. The shop was in a side street in a small part of the town centre that had been deemed of historical merit and spared from the bulldozers when the new shopping precinct and civic buildings were designed. Crawley's sold Gentleman's Relish and Bath Oliver biscuits. It was patronised by well-to-do retired people indulging nostalgia, prosperous middle-aged housewives who regarded its personal service and the sight of the delivery van at their doors as signs of their husband's success, and by modern young women who cooked with wine and enthusiasm and favoured the esoteric. Mr Crawley himself worked behind the counter, as his father and grandfather had done before him; his two women assistants had been there for years. Ray replaced an elderly driver who, after an operation, could no longer lift the order boxes. It was the best job he'd ever had, as things turned out, for he was his own boss when he was in the van, and by putting on speed in one area he won time to inspect another; he kew which customers were away because the weekly order wasn't given, and who was careless about locking up. He'd got into several empty houses and raised enough from what he found in them to buy the Imp. At all times he kept his eyes open, for you never knew.

He'd got the job at Crawley's through his mother, who was friendly with one of the women assistants. This personal link had been as good as a reference; Ray had come for his interview looking neat and tidy, and though he was younger than Mr Crawley really wanted his driver to be, his charm had carried the day. Ray knew how to turn it on when it was needed. He'd learned to drive during a brief spell with a builder.

One day he'd do a bank properly, a real hold-up with a gun; but that would need setting up. He'd need mates for it, probably. But when he got in with that sort of mob he'd have it made: a pad somewhere, and a long-legged bird to go with it. The thing was to work up to it gradually, without getting caught on the way. First, he must get himself out of Felsbury, which was only half-awake, to where it was all happening. He was vague about the exact nature of 'it'. He only knew that he needed excitement.

It would all take time, that was the pity. He must make sure that the drops, as he called the deposits, were regular events, and he would have to choose times when the streets were quiet. He hadn't yet worked out a scheme for overpowering his victims; he'd have to hit them over the head, he thought: not hard, just enough to stun them for a few minutes. He must choose depositors who were either old or fragile, small or female, or a combination of those requirements, so that they were easy to overcome; for that reason, when Ted Jessop dropped a bag at the bank one night, Ray did not follow him home. He was much too burly a fellow.

On Thursday evening Cecil was in his glass-paned office at the library checking returns of borrowing figures. Fiction was up again; it was always the most popular. The public libraries, begun as supports for education, now fulfilled an amenity function and it was hard, as a librarian, to see where the division lay. What was instruction to one reader might be relaxation to another. After a while he got up from his chair. He was rather stiff and his eyes ached; he would have to get them tested. He went out into the main library.

In front of the fiction shelves a row of readers pondered; there were several people reading in the reference section. Cecil felt a sense of ownership, looking about him. In time he would, indeed, be head librarian of such a library as this, if not, in fact, this very one. He might be a county librarian one day. He paced the aisles. The new girl, fresh from school, was on duty; he watched her putting books back in position and checked to see that she had done it correctly. It was surprising what trouble some people had in remembering alphabetical order. Inconsequentially, as he straightened a row, he recalled his first meeting with June. To this day he marvelled at the chance which had brought them together. He had not learned about Barry until some months after their wedding, when June's mother had mentioned it, thinking he already knew. She said that Barry lacked most of Cecil's qualities, and his prospects too; she preferred her daughter's second choice. Cecil did not understand how Barry could abandon June for someone else, but it explained why she had turned to him; his attitude towards her, always humble, grew less assured from that time onwards.

Someone spoke to him.

'Have you got *Mary, Queen of Scots*, by Antonia Fraser? I can't find it,' said a female voice.

Cecil turned, brought back to earth sharply from visions of June, and saw a thin, pale girl with hair in a coronet round her head.

'I expect it's out,' said Cecil. 'But I'll look on the shelf.'

Lorna followed him to the biography section.

'How silly of me – of course it's biography. I looked in history,' she said.

'It's out anyway,' said Cecil. 'Would you like to put in a card for it? I'm afraid it will cost you five pence.'

'Oh yes, I'll do that. Thank you,' said Lorna.

'You'll find cards over there, at the desk,' said Cecil, gesturing.

'Yes. Thank you,' said Lorna again.

She went towards the desk, and Cecil forgot her instantly. But they had met before. Lorna had once worked for an estate agent, and had come to the library to check on the history of a Jacobean house they were selling; Cecil had helped her find the details of it, even telephoning to the county library for her. Lorna had never forgotten the trouble he had taken; although she came into the library quite often they had not spoken again, but she had often seen him behind his glass partition.

She filled in the card, chose another book, and cycled back to her one-roomed flatlet, really a bed-sitter, over a paint-shop. Her journey took her past Tansy's Tea Shoppe, which was run by old Mr Beauchamp and his two daughters. The girls, as he called them, who were both in their forties, did the baking and most of the serving, while he washed up, took the money and balanced the books. He did most of the cleaning, too. She passed Crawley's, the grocer's, with its window displaying tinned chestnuts and whole Stiltons. Then she turned left and went past a travel bureau, a boutique, and Floradora's. The next turning, down a narrow street, led to an old block which housed, among other shops, the paint-shop; besides tins of emulsion and rolls of wallpaper, its window was full of do-it-yourself gadgetry and polystyrene tiles.

She reached her room by climbing past locked doors closed on sheeted cupboards, trunks and piles of bedsteads. Once, several other rooms in the building had been occupied, but they needed repair and redecoration, and as the leases expired they had been let again as furniture repositories. Lorna, alone, remained under the eaves, sole user of a dingy bathroom with a wayward geyser on the half-landing below her room. Occasionally people came from the furniture storers to remove or add to the goods stacked away, but most of the time only Lorna entered the building. There was just space for her bicycle in the narrow hall at the front of the staircase.

Her room contained a divan, an armchair, and the desk she had bought at a junk shop. At one end, a kitchen alcove was concealed by a curtain. A bright batik in red and purple hung on the wall above the divan, which was covered with a folkweave counterpane Lorna had bought in Majorca, where once she had gone on a package tour. Red, purple and orange cushions were heaped upon the divan, and there was a mock sheepskin rug on the floor. Rows of paperback books, whose titles ranged from *Jane Eyre* to *The Lost Tribes of the Kalahari*, filled low shelves on each side of the gas fire. Three vivid travel posters were pinned to another wall, and the curtains were printed with huge, exotic poppies. The whole room was a brilliant contradiction to the appearance its tenant presented to the world.

When she got back from the library, Lorna scrambled some eggs and ate an apple; she was not interested in cooking. Then she looked at her watch. It was still only half-past seven.

She changed from her navy skirt into a pair of jeans, unplaited her hair and fastened it back in a ponytail, put on a dark anorak, and then went downstairs.

The street lights were on, though it was not yet dark. Lorna mounted her bicycle and rode off.

Chapter 4

When June's class finished the following Tuesday evening Ted was waiting.

She had paid scant attention to the lesson. Whilst the class enquired of one another '*Come si chiama?*' her mind kept wandering away, wondering if he would be looking for her, and thinking, 'So what?' Nothing could happen. It was only a bit of fun.

Most of the pupils were older than June, but there was one other young woman. When they broke for five minutes halfway through, everyone chatted except her; she bent studiously over her textbook, and wrote new words in a small notebook.

'Hullo, there,' said Ted, when June appeared in the hall. He had no idea what she was studying so that he could not wait outside the appropriate room. He whiled away the time reading the lists on the board: keep fit, yoga, upholstery, musical appreciation: there was no end to the subjects you could learn.

He had been very busy in the last few days, with as much work as he could handle; he'd been to the airport this evening and had only just got back.

'Well, then?' What should he suggest? 'Would you like a drink?' he asked.

June had made a plan. Let Cecil fret if she were late; he'd never suspect the truth. She would say the car had refused to start, as in fact it had the week before.

'It'll have to be quick,' she said.

'All right. If you say so.'

They left her car where it was and got into the Humber. Ted drove to a friendly pub not far away, and they went into the snug where he bought her a gin and tonic. At first they simply sat and looked at one another, and then the laughter began again, the light, happy mirth that they had shared in the florist's.

'What are you studying?' June asked. He looked so neat in his navy-blue suit. She felt a curious excitement as she waited for his reply.

He told her the truth.

'Oh dear,' said June, when he had finished explaining. It was very flattering. He was watching her intently, wondering how she would respond, and her stomach seemed to give a lurch. Silently, she showed him her left hand.

He'd known, of course; she simply couldn't not be married. He took her hand in his, and from that instant they were both lost. As they walked out of the pub together June's knees felt weak; she was aware only of the bulk of him beside her, and of the sensations his closeness aroused. She hoped no one she knew would see them together; then she thought recklessly, I don't care if they do. They stopped at a telephone box on the corner and she rang Cecil. The car had refused to start, she said, but someone was fixing it. There was no need to worry.

Lorna saw Ted greet June in the hall of the college, and watched them leave together.

Ray had spent the early part of that evening watching a branch of Barclay's Bank in an outlying part of the town. He'd seen the safe used by a man from a tobacconist's shop, and a woman who kept a pet shop, but no one else. It was still light: reluctantly he realized that he would have to wait till the days grew shorter before he could act. He needed darkness. Meanwhile, the Imp had packed up: a big end, they'd said at the place he'd taken it to, and it would be a pricey job to fix it, so he needed money.

After a while he gave up his vigil. It was one thing to spend a couple of hours in the car, and quite another to stand lounging against a wall for everyone who passed to notice. He called in at a pub for a couple of beers, then started to walk back towards the centre of Felsbury. He might look in at the club, but it bored him; the disco left him unmoved, and they were all such kids. There was nothing to do here, that was the trouble. An hour at the new bowling alley was quite enough, though some people seemed happy to spend the whole evening there. And the birds were so dumb. He wanted one with a bit of class, like you saw on the films.

Ray had done well at school. His mother had wanted him to stay on and try for more 'O' levels, but he'd been fed up by that time and was keen to get out in the world. He'd started with an electrician, working as an apprentice on day-release, but he soon got bored and played truant when he was meant to be at the tech. His mother had never found out why he finally left; he'd spun her a tale about not getting on with the boss, and she'd accepted it. That was the end of his official education, but he'd learned a lot of other things since. He'd slipped in and out of jobs, sometimes working as a labourer, sometimes not working at all, but always bringing money home. He always worked alone, and so far he'd never got caught on a job.

At home, he was patient with his younger brothers and helped his mother with the chores; she thought him a model son and stifled the memory of when he had been sent home from school in disgrace, at the age of eight, for killing all the goldfish in the school's aquarium by putting disinfectant in the water. It was just a prank, she'd excused at the time, though his father thought differently and had taken his belt to the boy.

By the time Ray got to the new shopping precinct in the middle of the town it was dusk; at night the area around the shops was full of huddled bodies, clamped in pairs in doorways. As early as this the pairs had not yet formed, and the unromantic equivalent of the *passeggiata* was taking place. Groups of girls, giggling and preening themselves, loitered near the stairways, trying to attract the attention of the opposing groups of youths. Occasionally a burst of shrill laughter resounded along the covered walkways, or there was a sudden squeal as some sort of contact was made. Ray walked haughtily past a trio of girls who made loud remarks about his physical attributes as he went by. Silly cows. Serve them right if he was to do them one by one; it was what they were asking for. But it wasn't worth the bother. Girls like that were a waste of time. A vague image of someone like a mixture of the late Marilyn Monroe with touches of Liza Minnelli haunted his mind; she'd be kind of cushiony, and she'd smell of some exotic stuff, Turkish perhaps; she'd be languorous and stimulating, both at once, and she'd have these very long legs.

In the meantime, there was Brenda. When he'd nothing better to do he drove her out into the country in the Imp. She was always complaisant. She was small, thin and giggly, and she thought him a devil, but he fascinated her; she was sure they would marry one day, and so were her parents, who lived in a semi-detached house near the hospital and who thought him such a nice boy. They didn't know the half of it. Every time he and their daughter meshed in a tangle of limbs in the back of the Imp, or on the grass in some field, or in Brenda's room when her parents were out, he thought of the act as a triumph against them and their smug respectability. Till he could find something better, Brenda would do.

She was at home tonight; she'd washed her hair, thinking by nine o'clock that he wouldn't be coming that evening, and it was still damp. Her parents were in, watching television, just like his own.

He'd not got the car. It'd have to be the park.

Cecil had successfully fixed a flying buttress in position. He sat back to admire his work, which was set out on a large tray so that it was easily portable. The windows were a challenge; he used transparent film of different colours to give the impression of stained glass and he fixed a bulb inside, worked by a torch battery, so that they could be lighted to look like the real thing.

'Lovely, Daddy,' Janet always said when he arranged this sort of display, her soft little cheek pressed against his own face. She had his blue eyes and June's rich, tawny hair, and her nose was dusted with freckles. He worshipped her.

June's telephone call about the car had disturbed his tranquillity. It should not have refused to start; he saw to its maintenance regularly. She had been vague about the nature of the trouble but seemed calm. It was lucky that there were people about to help her; at least it had not broken down on the way home. She would still want tea when she got back.

He put the kettle on and laid the tray, as he always did on Tuesdays. A little cry came from upstairs: Barty with a dream. The small boy lay in his bed clutching a stuffed giraffe to his heart and whimpering with fright. Cecil soothed him and sat with him for a while till he fell asleep again.

The watcher across the way saw him go out of the room, then return to his model-making. June came back more than an hour after her usual time; she was smiling and animated, gesturing with her arms and talking fast. Suddenly she flung herself against Cecil and embraced him ardently. The watcher saw his arms go round her and their two bodies lock. Very soon after that the lights went out.

Ray could scarcely believe his luck when, after he'd taken Brenda home and was walking back past the post office, he saw a man with a bag approaching the Midland Bank. It was late by now, and there were few people about. The pubs had closed; there was nothing to stay out for, in Felsbury.

Ray looked around. He was in full view of the street lights, but there were no pedestrians near, and no traffic in sight, though some cars were parked at the kerb.

Bert Walsh, temporary landlord of The Feathers, sent in by the brewery during the real landlord's absence on holiday, never liked having cash on the place at night, unlike the man he was replacing, who took it up to his bedroom after locking up. He was fumbling with the key of the safe when his feet were suddenly jerked from under him and he went over like a nine-pin, struck his head against the wall and was knocked out cold. Ray had hooked a foot round his ankle and jerked him over. He seized the leather bag and was off round the corner, haring up the road minutes before anyone realized that something was wrong. Even then, a passer-by, seeing Bert Walsh lying on the ground, thought he must have had some sort of attack. Not till Walsh came round in hospital and was able to explain what had happened was the money missed. By that time Ray was well away and had opened the bag. It contained over £200.

Chapter 5

Mrs Malmesbury was recovering. Hesther Ford, whom she sometimes met for lunch and who lived not far from Felsbury, had been to the flat to collect the personal things she wanted. Though even older than Mrs Malmesbury, Mrs Ford was more spry; she was very deaf, but energetic, and scampered everywhere in a sort of run so that Mrs Malmesbury feared she would one day fall and break her hip. Luckily, she herself had broken no bones in her own tumble. She was to stay with Mrs Ford when she left hospital, until she felt able to return to Cleveland Court.

Mrs Malmesbury had no recollection at all of what had happened in the library; her last memory was of leaving Mr Vigors' surgery. She was very surprised when, a week after she had collapsed, a young man from the library came to see her. She recognized him; he was one of the more senior people, she knew; seldom to be seen actually in the library but often visible behind the glass partition.

He was slightly built, of moderate height, with thinning hair and blue eyes; rather a solemn young man, as she told Mrs Ford later. She was touched at his coming.

'I must have caused you so much trouble,' she apologised. 'Fainting in the library! What a thing to do!'

'I'm glad you're better,' said Cecil. He had brought her another book for which she had asked some time ago.

'It must have been you who brought Emmeline

Pankhurst for me,' said Mrs Malmesbury. 'You are kind.'
She hadn't felt like tackling Mrs Pankhurst yet; the book
he had brought today looked more suitable for someone
ill: it was the new Pamela Hansford Johnson. Mrs
Malmesbury hoped the young man would not stay too
long, so that she might begin it.

Cecil had called in rather on the spur of the moment,
and found that, because she was in a side ward, Mrs
Malmesbury was allowed visitors at any time. Miss Binks
had come into his office carrying the book and saying that
it was Mrs Malmesbury's turn to have it; what should be
done, she wanted to know.

'Seeing that she's ill,' Miss Binks had added, and Cecil,
irritated by the girl's officious tone, had said shortly that
he would take it to her.

Cecil was accustomed to hospitals and did not mind
going to them. He had never been ill himself, but Janet
and Barty had both been born at Snettlesham General,
and his mother had died in another hospital after a long
illness during which he had visited her every day. The
smells of polish, disinfectant and mass-cooked food did
not upset him; nor did the nurses.

Cecil talked about Mrs Pankhurst while Mrs Malmesbury
listened, hoping he would not catch her out in having so
far not read the book.

'I haven't finished it,' she truthfully said, in case he
expected to bear it away with him. 'But I won't be long
now – I'm feeling so much better.'

Indeed, she looked quite bright, sitting propped up by
pillows, wearing a pretty frilled bed-jacket buttoned up to
her chin.

Cecil had been there just a few minutes when a nurse
appeared.

'Another visitor for you, Mrs Malmesbury,' she said.
'You are popular today.'

It was Lorna Gibson.

Mrs Malmesbury stared at her blankly; she did not recognize her. Hyper-sensitive, Lorna realized it at once and the slow colour came into her face. Cecil, who stood up when she came in, looked at her in a puzzled way. Her face was familiar but he could not place her; a library user, of course.

'I'm Mr Vigors' receptionist. You don't remember me,' said Lorna flatly. 'Mr Vigors asked me to come and see how you were getting on. He – we were so sorry to hear you were ill.'

'How very kind,' said Mrs Malmesbury. 'I'm being made such a fuss of, I shan't want to go home. Now, let me see, Mr Er – ? You haven't met have you?'

'Titmuss. Cecil Titmuss,' he supplied, and Lorna spoke swiftly, before he could agree that they had not.

'We have, at the library. My name's Lorna Gibson.'

'Of course I remember. Mary, Queen of Scots,' said Cecil, inspired, and saw Lorna blush again, this time with amazed pleasure.

She had dreaded this visit. Only Mr Vigors' stern insistence had given her the power to come at all. She was afraid of illness and its attendant paraphernalia. At her protest, Vigors had said that if she felt unable to carry out this request, then it showed she was unsuited to her job.

'You lack warmth, Lorna,' he said.

'How cruel of you, Bryan,' said Susan later when he related this.

'Well, she took in what I said and went off to the hospital straight away. She doesn't want to leave. Funny, I don't know why she stays. I'd have thought she'd have preferred an office job – something less personal.'

'She hasn't to bother about other people with you and Nancy,' said Susan sagely. 'You're both easy to get along with. In an office, the work might be impersonal, but there'd be other girls; she'd have to make a bit more effort. She's a loner. I'm sorry for her.'

Now, Lorna sat on one side of Mrs Malmesbury's high bed while Cecil sat on the other, and the old lady asked them both about themselves. If she could get them to talk, she need make little conversation herself, and perhaps they would soon go. She was tired, although she was so much better. The day was quite full, with nurses making her get out of bed so that her lungs kept clear, and the physiotherapist treating her briskly; there wasn't much peace.

Cecil willingly talked about his children. Lorna had less to say, just that she enjoyed her job. No, she had not worked for a dentist before.

They left together – or rather, Cecil got up to leave and Lorna followed him.

Mrs Malmesbury managed to thank them both with some effusiveness, and stay awake till they had left the room. Pamela Hansford Johnson would have to wait till later.

Lorna and Cecil walked together along the corridor past signs pointing to X-ray, out-patients, casualty and so forth. People walked briskly about: doctors in white coats, and nurses; no one loitered. Lorna shuddered slightly.

'I don't like hospitals,' she said.

'People do get better, you know,' said Cecil. 'Like Mrs Malmesbury. She'll soon be discharged.'

'I know. But you give up being responsible for yourself, when you're ill.'

A porter pushing a trolley came towards them; an unconscious man lay on it, and a nurse walked at his side. Cecil and Lorna moved close to the wall to let the little procession go past. The patient's face was grey.

'There. You see?' said Lorna.

'He's probably only had his appendix out,' said Cecil. As they moved out of the way of the trolley, his arm had brushed against Lorna's; Cecil had not noticed the slight contact, but Lorna had felt the rough touch of his jacket. She did not draw away. Now, as he spoke, Cecil looked at her, and saw that she was almost as pale as the man on the trolley. 'You really do mind, don't you? How do you manage to work for a dentist if you get upset like this?' he asked.

'People don't often faint at the dentist's,' said Lorna. 'And if they do, they soon recover. Besides, the other girl does most of the chair-side work. I'm usually in the office.'

'It seems odd work for you to choose, all the same.'

'It's different,' she said. 'And it's quiet, in the office. You can get on with the work in your own way, peacefully.'

'Why don't you like hospitals? Have you been ill yourself?'

She had not even got that excuse.

'I see what you mean about surrendering your responsibility,' said Cecil. 'But if a person is ill enough, he's past caring. It was brave of you to visit Mrs Malmesbury, though, feeling as you do. She's a nice old lady.'

'Yes,' said Lorna, who had in fact been too busy thinking about herself to give much thought to the patient.

'She must be lonely,' said Cecil. He saw plenty of lonely people in the library, and they were by no means all old.

'She might be, I suppose,' said Lorna, who had not thought of such a possibility.

They emerged from the hospital.

'Well, I go this way,' said Cecil, turning to the left. His car, securely locked, was behind the maternity block. 'Goodbye.'

He did not ask which way Lorna was going, but strode

off, hurrying home to June and the children. Lorna watched him till he vanished round the corner. Then, more slowly, she walked away in the other direction.

Ray gloated over his prize. He kept the money in an old cocoa tin under a floorboard in his room; he couldn't trust his mother not to go through his drawers when she put his washing away. It had been so easy. That quick hook round the old fellow's ankle had been just right. It'd work with a woman – though she might scream. He wondered, now, looking back, why the old man hadn't yelled; fright, maybe. Another time Ray intended to wear a mask; he'd got an old stocking that his mother had thrown in the dustbin. It smelled faintly female and musty; he put it on sometimes and grimaced at himself in the mirror, practising fierce expressions. Once, when he'd got it on, his brother Doug had come to his room wanting something; Ray had nearly bitten the boy's head off, grabbing at the mask and turning his back to the door as the child came in.

He had decided that one of the victims must be the blonde from Floradora's. He'd been in to the florist's to reconnoitre. She wasn't there that day, but there was a bird in charge, rather old for him but the sort he fancied and meant to get for himself once he got away from Felsbury. She was long-legged, with large breasts, different from Brenda's little buttons. Chestnut hair, she'd got, too, kind of wavy, and big golden-brown eyes. He'd bought some violets.

'For me mum,' he said. He'd chucked them in the gutter later.

The bird had opened the till and Ray had seen wads of notes inside it: whole stacks of fivers under a clamp, and tenners too, besides the singles. It was just asking to be nicked. Another day he went to Tansy's Tea Shoppe and had a cream tea. Because he always looked neat and kept his hair cut to just below his ears in a tidy bob, no one in Tansy's looked askance at him. He'd done this on a Saturday afternoon; no deliveries were made then though Crawley's was open. Ray worked on Wednesday afternoons instead, when the shop was closed. Tansy's till was well filled too, Ray saw. Those two would bring in a fair bit between them, and if he got the chance, he'd do another job. Then he'd be off.

Meanwhile, he got the Imp fixed. He'd found this repair workshop near the gas works; the guy there seemed to know what he was doing and quoted what sounded to Ray a reasonable price. When he went to fetch the car there was another bloke there, working on a big black Humber.

'Out of the ark, isn't it?' Ray asked, as the man crawled out from under the old car, wiping his hands on an oily rag. He was a thickset fellow with dark, curly hair.

'Built to last,' said the man, patting the car as if it were human. 'Come for your Imp, have you? Charlie said you'd be round.' And he said not to let the lad take it without getting the money. 'It's all yours. Shouldn't have any more bother.'

Ray peeled the money off a wad of five-pound notes which he took from his denim jacket pocket, and counted them out. There were plenty left.

'I'll give you a receipt,' said Ted.

Ray waited while he made it out. Mr Ray Brett, wrote Ted methodically, and the address of the Bretts' flat on the other side of Felsbury.

The following Tuesday Ted was waiting when June arrived at the college. By the time she had parked the car he was standing beside it.

They looked at one another in silence for a long moment. Then Ted opened the door, took her by the elbow, and without a word they left the college yard together. The Humber was parked round the corner; it took less than five minutes to drive to the mews where Ted lived.

For him there was no choice; of course she was married. And he'd got this sort of jinx which seemed to protect him from the charms of unmarried girls; this kind of thing had happened before, and there were advantages. You were saved from commitment, which he couldn't afford. But June was special; he knew it instantly, and her hunger for him increased his own eagerness. She assured him that Cecil would never question where she was on Tuesday evenings; they could meet every week. Neither she nor Ted looked further ahead, at this point, than their next meeting.

June found it hard to believe that this was happening to her. The moment she entered Ted's room she became a different person, shedding her mantle of rectitude with the same abandon as she discarded her clothes and cast them into an untidy heap on the floor. She scarcely noticed her surroundings: the sparsely furnished room with just a divan, a worn armchair, a table with diary, telephone directory and account book on the top of it, and the gas stove where Ted cooked his meals, all in such contrast to The Lindens, where over the years hard work and good taste had created a very different setting. She was aware only of Ted, and her own response to him; for the present nothing else mattered.

Lorna, arriving for her third Italian lesson, saw them again. The next week, when June did not come at all, Lorna too abandoned the lesson.

June and Cecil Titmuss's house, The Lindens, was on the corner of Masterton Road, separated from the street by a small garden and a fence. Lorna, bicycling past, saw that the garage door was open and the car was out. She turned left, into Western Grove. Here the houses were tall and terraced; their gardens were small, not much bigger than yards, and those of numbers Twenty-Four and Twenty-Six both bordered the much bigger garden of The Lindens. She rode the whole length of the street, then back again. It was quiet; most of the houses in Western Grove were now offices, though a few were let as flats. She went into a telephone box at the end of the road and consulted the yellow pages. Under the headings of both 'Car Hire' and 'Taxis' there were a great many entries. Mrs Malmesbury had not mentioned the taxi-driver's name; finding it out might prove to be quite difficult.

By now it was almost dark. Lorna cycled back to Western Grove, where she chained her bicycle against some iron railings where thick bushes thrust through, so that the machine was half-concealed. Then she walked swiftly down the road and stopped at number Twenty-Six. Here, she was out of the immediate pool of light cast by the street lamp on the corner; dimly, the two brass plates on the door gleamed. Lorna fitted a key into the lock, swung the door open and slipped inside. She did not turn on the light, but felt her way upstairs with the familiarity of one who had done it many times before. The house was hushed, with the total stillness of emptiness. Lorna crossed the landing and went into a room at the back of the house, hurrying to the window.

Cecil had not drawn the curtains. She could see him seated at a table; the little girl faced him, and the small boy was by his side. They were playing some sort of game, ludo perhaps, or halma.

Lorna unlocked her personal drawer in the desk; she and Nancy each had one, but Nancy's was never locked. From a small leather case, also locked, Lorna took out a pair of binoculars. She trained them on the little scene in the neighbouring house. Cecil was intent on the game and the children; she saw him guide the small boy as he moved a piece. They played for some time before Cecil took the children up to bed, and Lorna stayed by the window, in the darkness of Bryan Vigors' office, watching them. She was still there when June came back, much later.

Chapter 6

'Will you really be all right, Dorothy?'

Mrs Ford was anxious. Mrs Malmesbury had been discharged from hospital ten days ago; Ted Jessop had brought her to Diddington, the village six miles from Felsbury where the Fords lived, to spend a period of convalescence, and now she had returned home, driven this time by Mrs Ford. A message to the woman who came two mornings a week to do the cleaning had ensured that milk, bread, and a frozen chicken dinner were waiting. Now Mrs Ford was reluctant to leave her old friend, who still looked frail.

'Of course I will, Hesther. I must start to do things for myself again, you know,' said Mrs Malmesbury.

'I wish I could stay for a day or two, and just settle you in.' Mrs Ford hovered, irresolute, in the doorway of the flat. 'You'll telephone at once, if you'd like to come back? Or if you feel ill again?'

'I promise.'

'If it wasn't for Edgar – ' Mrs Ford did not finish. Her husband was ninety-five. His memory was poor, but physically he was surprisingly fit. He went for walks and forgot where he lived, and was a perpetual anxiety to his wife. On the days when she met Mrs Malmesbury in Felsbury she worried constantly about what Edgar would be doing while her back was turned. Once he had been brought home by a child of eight who had met him wandering about; she took him by the hand, and led him back while he told her about the relief of Mafeking, where he had been as a very young man, and of which she had naturally enough never heard.

'Off you go, Hesther.' Mrs Malmesbury, would, in fact, not be able to endure her friend's departure if she did not go soon. 'Drive carefully. And thank you.'

Mrs Malmesbury laid her papery cheek against that of Mrs Ford, and watched her walk down the passage towards the lift. Then she closed the door and limped over to the window; her arthritis was less painful after the prolonged rest, but she was very stiff. She was in time to see Mrs Ford emerge from the building and dart over to her car, a mustard-coloured Mini. She got in and drove off with a flourish; she drove as she did everything else: with energy.

Mrs Malmesbury turned away from the window. She felt desolate. She was quite alone, and if she had another attack no one would know until Mrs Brett came next time. She rubbed at her eyes and shook herself crossly; it was foolish to think like that. Hesther would telephone this evening, and again tomorrow; she was lucky to have such a friend. She sat down in her armchair and put her foot up on a stool covered in her own *gros point*. She still worked at her tapestries.

In her mind she followed Hesther back to Diddington. She hoped that Edgar would not have roamed away again. To think that he had once commanded a brigade o cavalry: he had been decorated several times and was one of the handsomest men she had ever met; now he was like a shuffling old tortoise.

She dropped off to sleep.

The doorbell woke her. She had been dreaming: she and Hesther were at a ball, she wearing white and Hesther in yellow; they had been waltzing with two army officers, Edgar Ford and Duncan Malmesbury. She sighed, making an effort to return to the present. She had been in love with Edgar as a girl, and had remained in love with him after he had married Hesther, even after Duncan's constancy had won her over. She had never regretted her marriage, and she was glad now that Duncan had died before he too became a shambling wreck like Edgar.

The bell rang again. She got up and hobbled to the door.

A plain, dark girl stood outside, clutching a bunch of miniature roses. Mrs Malmesbury knew her. She struggled to think of her name.

The girl looked ill at ease.

'Oh – Mrs Malmesbury – are you better? I brought you these,' said Lorna awkwardly, thrusting the flowers at the old lady.

'How very kind.' Mrs Malmesbury racked her brains in an effort to place the girl. If she could bluff it out for a few minutes, she might remember. Did she work in some shop? They had met recently, she felt certain: in hospital. Was she a nurse? It was something along those lines, Mrs Malmesbury was sure. The dentist – that was it. She was Mr Vigors' receptionist. Relief made Mrs Malmesbury warm in her welcome. 'Come in, my dear,' she said. If she offered the girl tea, or some sherry, she need not be alone for a while. 'I'm quite well again,' she said, leading the way to the sitting-room. 'I've been to stay with a friend.'

It was five o'clock now, and getting dark already; the evenings were drawing in. Mrs Malmesbury drew the curtains across the windows and turned to her visitor, who still grasped the flowers.

'What beautiful roses.' Were they from the girl or from Mr Vigors? How difficult to know. 'Thank you so much.' That was the right thing to say, whatever the answer.

'Shall I find a vase?' offered Lorna. The old lady was teetering back and forth where she stood; if she didn't soon sit, she would fall.

'Yes, please,' said Mrs Malmesbury, and explained where they were kept.

She sat down, while Lorna arranged the flowers carefully; she had bought them at Floradora's the evening before, when they were tight buds, and now they were fully open. She'd meant to come round to see Mrs Malmesbury sooner, but it had taken her all day to summon enough courage.

'Let's have some sherry,' said Mrs Malmesbury, when the job was done. 'In the cupboard over there, my dear. And the glasses are in the kitchen.' She couldn't remember the girl's name, but it didn't matter.

Lorna fetched decanter and glasses, and poured out the sherry. They sat in silence, neither able to think of any topic to discuss. But the senior lady had an active social sense.

'How good of you to come over on a Sunday. What do you usually do on Sundays?' she asked.

Lorna sometimes went to concerts. In fine weather she bicycled about the countryside and looked at churches.

Mrs Malmesbury enquired if she had been to Diddington, where there was a church dating from Norman times, with a crusader's tomb. Lorna had not.

'When did you come home?' she asked Mrs Malmesbury. The old lady looked very frail; her skin was translucent, like wax, and huge veins stood out on her hands; the joints of her fingers were swollen. An obscure emotion, which Lorna did not recognize but which in fact was pity, stirred the girl.

'This afternoon. My friend drove me. Then she had to hurry back to her husband. He's incredibly old, even older than I am,' said Mrs Malmesbury, and chuckled a little.

'You came by car to see Mr Vigors,' said Lorna tentatively. Here was her chance.

'Ah yes – Ted Jessop – such a find. Such a nice young man. He drives me to the shops every Tuesday – or he did, before my accident,' said Mrs Malmesbury.

It was as easy as that. Lorna had got the name that she had come for, but she stayed a little longer. She washed up the sherry glasses and even asked if Mrs Malmesbury could manage to get her own supper.

'Oh yes,' said Mrs Malmesbury. 'It's all frozen. I need only switch on the oven. How nice of you to call, my dear. Come again, if you're passing and have the time.'

'I will,' said Lorna, and crossed her fingers.

When she left the flat she raced along the corridor and ran down the stairs, ignoring the lift. She could not wait to escape from that atmosphere: the old lady had nothing to do but wait for death. And nor had she, at twenty-nine: Lorna Gibson, spinster, had no life of her own and no aim except to gaze from a window at the life of another, and wish herself part of it.

On Sundays Cecil cleaned the car, and in fine weather he worked in the garden. Sometimes he took the children to church, and was disappointed if June stayed away. He felt proud when he was able to usher his whole family before him into a pew.

June had become more beautiful than ever lately; he would never have believed that going back to work could make such a difference. He knew that the company of various young women whose children went to school with Janet and Barty bored her; he had tried to talk to her about library matters and events in the town in an interesting way, but his companionship in the evenings was evidently not enough for her. They went, occasionally, to concerts and lectures, chosen usually because Cecil thought he ought to be there in his role as deputy librarian; but it was never easy to get a reliable baby-sitter. Sometimes they went to the cinema, though Cecil thought that the films June wanted to see were rather upsetting. He was a little upset himself just now; June had grown so radiant that it was difficult for him not to keep telling her so, and he did not always succeed, with the result that their love-making had strayed away from the weekends and sometimes took place in the middle of the week too, for which Cecil felt apologetic.

On the Sunday that Lorna visited Mrs Malmesbury, the Titmuss family spent the day with June's parents. Once every five or six weeks they made this expedition, always eating so much rich food that Cecil felt liverish afterwards and could not understand why his father-in-law had not perished long ago from too much cholesterol. This time, June's mother commented on her glowing appearance and asked if she were pregnant.

June denied it at once.

'You look so well. You've been peaky all summer,' said her mother.

'It's the job. It's good for me to get out,' said June.

'I'm sure I don't know how you do it. It kept me busy enough, looking after your brother and you, and your father,' said her mother.

'The money's handy,' said June shortly. Her mother noticed too much. June was glad when it was time to leave.

As they passed through the centre of Felsbury on the way home their route took them past the church in the town centre. The mayor's car was parked outside it; some official service was going on and a lot of people were trooping through the big west doors. Among the cars parked behind that of the mayor June recognized Ted's Humber, and there he was, standing beside it in his navy suit, wearing his peaked cap. June felt her cheeks begin to burn. They drove past and she looked right at Ted; for a moment he saw her staring at him from the front of the Morris. To him, the figure of Cecil beside her was a blur, and he was only dimly aware of the children in the back of the car. Then they were gone.

It was hairwash night for Janet. While she and June were upstairs, Cecil made Barty read to him; the child was not getting on fast enough at school, he felt: some individual attention was needed. Later, when both children were in bed, he and June watched television, Cecil with divided concentration for he was working on Notre Dame. The play was about Spain, and bullfights. June seemed to be enjoying it, though Cecil thought it trite; gradually he stopped even listening to it.

June was not attending either. She was far away in her thoughts. Seeing Ted like that, so suddenly, had been disturbing. He lived in uncomfortable conditions, and the bed where they made love was narrow and lumpy, but he was exciting and he had made her come alive. Cecil was like a man of fifty already; he had been born middle-aged. Where would it all end? It could not go on like this for ever, she supposed, but whatever the future she could not draw back now. In a moment of insight she knew that if it had not been Ted, it would have been someone else, given the opportunity.

Across the way, Lorna was at her post. She had arrived, having cycled from Mrs Malmesbury's, just after the family got back from their day out, and she saw their movements about the house. The dining-room was not overlooked from the road, and the houses that bordered the garden were all used as business premises and therefore assumed to be empty out of office hours, so that the curtains were often left open until late. June saw Cecil and Barty with their book, Janet drying her hair, and the woman who made up the quartet moving among them as if there was no secret treachery which she must conceal.

Lorna hated her.

Ray and Brenda spent that Sunday in Weston-super-Mare. The Imp hummed along, its engine sweet after the ministrations it had received. They went on to the pier and gazed at the Bristol Channel, bathed in murk as it was on this overcast day, and had lunch in a café on the front where the smell of fat hung in the air. Afterwards they went to the cinema, and drove home in the dark, stopping on the way to pull well off the road into a copse.

It was cramped in the back of the car, and Brenda said so.

'When're we going to get married, Ray?' she asked, pulling down her skirt. 'I'm tired of this, grubbing in cars and the park.'

'Who said anything about getting married?' Ray was horrified at the idea. 'I never.'

'Well, you meant it, didn't you? Stands to reason,' said Brenda. 'We can afford it, can't we? If I kept on me job.' Brenda worked at a supermarket check-out.

'Where'd we live?' Ray parried.

'We'd find something. We could start off at my place. Mum and Dad wouldn't mind.'

'No thanks,' said Ray. 'We're not getting married, and that's that.'

There was no mistaking his tone, and Brenda was dismayed. She'd always thought they would, one day. Ray had a steady job and his parents were decent folk, approved by hers.

'I'd never've –' Brenda began.

'Oh yes, you would, my girl,' said Ray, and his voice was steely. 'You were good and ready. Don't give me that one.' He got out of the back of the car and slid in behind the steering wheel. 'Get moving, if you want to come in front.'

Muttering under her breath, Brenda obeyed. He started the engine and drove off with a jerk before she was settled. She began to snivel.

'Oh Ray! And I thought we –'

'Cut that out, you silly cow,' he said, putting his foot down hard.

He did not speak again till they reached the end of the street where she lived.

'That's as far as I'm coming,' he snapped, leaning across her and opening the passenger's door. 'Get out.'

'But Ray –' she began to plead.

'Stop that whining and get out. We're through,' said Ray, remembering how they dealt with these things in films.

Brenda cringed.

'Ray, I'm sorry –' she whimpered.

He bundled her out of the car without another word, pushing her thin body so that she half fell to the pavement. Then he slammed the door and she stumbled away. Without another word, he drove off. Brenda went weeping down the road and let herself in by the back door, hoping not to be heard above the television, but in vain. Her mother followed her upstairs and found her sobbing on her bed.

'Had a tiff have you, you and Ray? Well, don't take on. It'll all come right,' her mother comforted. 'You'll get over it, both of you.'

For it was time Brenda got married, and there was nothing wrong with Ray; lovers' quarrels were only to be expected.

Though Cecil did not remember it, Lorna had first seen him some time before they met in the library. She had been working for the estate agent through whom he bought The Lindens. Cecil had called at the office and Mr Grimes had given him particulars of various houses; over the next weeks he had come in several times and Lorna had learned that he was taking up a post at the library. The houses he saw were never quite right; either the price was too high or the garden too small. Then he had seen The Lindens, which was empty. It was an executor's sale, and Lorna had shown several people round the ugly house with its large, high-ceilinged rooms. She had liked it. Looking up at a neighbouring house, one day, she had seen a figure at a window peering across.

'It's overlooked,' said the client she was with, and he had gone no further.

But when Cecil raised the same point Mr Grimes explained that the houses which bordered the garden were all business premises. He sent Lorna to find out specifically what they were, and she saw Mr Vigors' and Mr Carruthers' plates on the door of Twenty-Six, Western Grove. Number Twenty-Four housed a solicitor, and next to him was an optician and an accountant. No one would overlook The Lindens at weekends. Cecil had bought the house; he could put down a good deposit, for his mother had recently died and left him her small estate.

That had been several years ago. Lorna had seen Cecil in the library constantly, and then they had their consultation about the house she was checking on. The dreams began gradually, and were spasmodic to begin with, for at that time she still hoped to break out somehow from behind her barrier of withdrawal. She went on a package tour to Majorca, but spent the whole holiday alone until an elderly couple in the same hotel took pity on her and asked her to join them on various excursions. She joined a badminton club, and though she played quite well, she was tongue-tied off the court; the other players gave up trying with her in the end, when she managed only monosyllabic answers to their friendly overtures. She even got as far as going to the doctor to ask for help, but had been unable to explain what was wrong. He, a busy man with his surgery full of mothers and babies and chronic bronchitics, felt exasperated with her. He prescribed tranquillizers, since she'd managed to complain of being edgy, and made no further effort to understand her problems.

She swallowed a few of the pills, but they seemed to make no difference, so she forgot about the rest. Slowly she grew more and more self-contained. She read a great deal, both fact and fiction; some of what she read alarmed her, the rest lulled. She began to dream of a shadowy someone, not defined but vaguely male, who would treat her with so much unspecified tenderness that she would magically be freed from her invisible prison and able to communicate. But this paragon never appeared; instead, after badminton one week, Eric Sims, aged thirty-three, had walked her home. He was known as a randy fellow, but not by Lorna, who did not know the word. Behind her back, the members of the badminton club had talked about her in despair.

'What she needs is a bit of you-know-what,' one of the men had said, over a beer, to the titters of the women.

'Right, Eric. Just the job for you,' they said to him. So Eric, as if embarking on a crusade, had accepted the challenge.

He took her to her door and then said, 'How about asking me up for a coffee?'

Gruffly, Lorna answered, 'All right, if you want one,' thinking that he did.

He followed her up the steep stairs. She looked all right from behind; her figure was good. And he'd been quite surprised at her room, when they reached it, with its bright furnishings and vivid posters. There must be another side to her nature; these quiet ones were like that.

She went to put the kettle on, and returned through the curtains into the main part of the room. Because of the recent exercise she was slightly flushed, and her hair, though tied back in a pony-tail, was not as neat as usual: a few loose wisps framed her face. She didn't look too bad at all.

68

Before Lorna realized what was happening, Eric had grabbed her. Hard lips were forced against hers, and she thought she would choke as an enormous tongue was forced into her mouth and down her throat, as it seemed. She was convinced he had gone completely mad; terror gave her enough strength to break free and she seized a chair which she held up before her like a shield.

'Get out!' she cried. 'Get out, get out!'

'Now wait a minute, Lorna. Cool it, can't you?' Eric tried to salvage some dignity. As she faced him, eyes blazing, the chair wavering in her grasp, he felt genuine desire. 'I didn't mean to scare you,' he said, for it was clear that she was really frightened.

He took a step backwards, and she set the chair down between them.

'Just go,' she said, and now her face was white.

Well, it was no good if you had to beg for it. There were plenty of other girls. Eric left.

Lorna never played badminton again.

Her parents had lived in Yorkshire, in a village on the edge of the moors where her father kept a pub. Her mother helped in the bar and cooked snack meals. Every night, but particularly on Saturdays, her father drank heavily; sometimes, Lorna would wake in the night, not knowing what had disturbed her, and would hear her mother crying. As she grew older, she began to understand the reason. Her mother grew thinner and more faded; she was often bruised about the face.

In spite of the landlord, patrons still came to the pub, for there was not another one for miles; one of them, a commercial traveller from Leeds, rescued Lorna's mother. He took her away, and the girl was left while the father roared about the place like a madman. Soon, though, he appeared with a strapping blonde whom he installed, officially, as housekeeper. She was more than he bargained for, and she managed to tame him. But Lorna withdrew into the shadows, waiting until her mother should send for her, for surely she would.

But she did not. And then she and the commercial traveller were killed in a car smash.

Lorna stayed on, quieter than ever, and when she left school she began to work in the bar. She was paid only pocket money. One day she stole fifty pounds from the till and ran away to London, where she found a room in a hostel and a job in a shop. At first she was terrified in case her father hunted her down because of the money she had taken. After some time, when nothing happened, she grew calmer, and as soon as she had managed to save fifty pounds from her wages she posted it to him by registered mail.

With this hurdle passed, she took stock and decided that she must acquire some specific training, so she began to study shorthand and typing at evening classes. This solved, too, the problem of how to occupy her time when she was not at work, for she was unable to mix easily with girls she met at the hostel or in the shop. She travelled about on buses on Sundays, and in that way discovered Felsbury. She missed the country; London was a lonely place if one was shy; as soon as she had passed her exams she moved. Life was cheaper in a provincial town, and more friendly, she had heard.

Her financial circumstances improved immediately, but her social life continued as before, though she made various efforts to break out of her isolation. But after her meeting in the library with Cecil, when he was patient with her queries, her vague daydreams took more definite shape; the identity of the person who would save her from her loneliness took on his likeness. Whenever she went to the library, she looked for him; she took to cycling past The Lindens in the hope of seeing him, and was occasionally rewarded by the sight of him washing the car. Then she saw the job with Mr Vigors advertised. She applied, and got it.

Mr Grimes was disappointed when she left; she had a future with the firm, he said.

Lorna's salary with Mr Vigors was less than she had been earning, and there were no promotion prospects, but she was satisfied; her life was simple and she was not extravagant. She had found the room above the paint-shop when she was working for Mr Grimes, and that had been a lucky discovery, for it suited her perfectly to be alone in the building, as she was. She had a key to the surgery, for she arrived before Mr Vigors every morning to see to the mail; and the cleaning woman, who also came early, had another. At first she was content merely to watch June Titmuss and the children in the garden, during the day; she identified with the other girl and was vicariously warmed by the domestic contentment she supposed existed within The Lindens. Once, by chance, she saw Cecil at the table making one of his models, when the room was lit; he must have had a day off, or come home early from the library. Then she realized what she could do, and her night visits began. They started in the summer; watching patiently, she saw the lights come on and the play begin; her intent had nothing of the sexual *voyeuse* about it; she was simply absorbed, like a theatre-goer, in the life unfolding before her, seeking to be a part of it. Sometimes, on Sundays, she spent whole days in the office. Standing well back from the window, she would see Cecil and the children in the garden. She knew that Mr Vigors would never come to the surgery then; he said often enough that he left his work behind on Friday night or the few Saturdays he worked. He was wrapped up, as she thought Cecil must be too, in his wife and family.

Once, Mr Carruthers, the chiropodist, came in when she was in the office. She froze, motionless, above. He did not come upstairs but soon left again carrying some papers.

In any case, she could always say, if found there, that she had remembered something she'd neglected to do and come to rectify it.

Chapter 7

Ted had turned down several Tuesday bookings so that he could meet June. It was folly, when every pound counted, but there was no other time when he could see her. By now she was not only a delight, but a habit, and familiarity had increased their pleasure in one another.

He heard her arrive, and was down the stairs before she had finished parking. She scraped the gears, getting into reverse; he was amused at himself for not minding her poor performance as a driver.

'Shows you've got it bad, my lad,' he told himself.

June was already beginning to wonder how they would manage when the Italian classes stopped for the Christmas break; she would have no excuse for going out. At Easter the course ceased altogether, but that was too far off to worry about yet. Perhaps they could sometimes meet in the afternoons, she thought, staring at the flaking plaster on the ceiling of Ted's room. There were cobwebs up there.

Down in the darkness of the mews Lorna saw the Morris parked, and the light in the window behind the thin curtains. She must be certain. She shivered, standing there; it was early November now and the weather was cold. What was happening inside that building? Her imagination transcribed scenes she had seen in films, casting Ted and June in the leading roles; it made her feel rather sick. While all this was going on Cecil, quite unaware, was quietly working away at that model of his.

At five past nine the door at the top of the stairs opened

and two figures showed up black against the sudden oblong of light. They both came down; June got into her car, and drove off with a roar of too much choke. Lorna shrank back into a dark patch of shadow where she could not be seen. When the car had gone she pulled her bicycle out of a nearby gateway and rode off. As she pedalled along a lump rose in her throat and she began to cry, soundlessly. She did not know why she wept; perhaps her tears were for Cecil, so easily deceived; perhaps they were for herself.

June's scent still hung in the air in Ted's room; she had left her scarf. He picked it up. He wished she came more often; life was a lonely business, and for the first time in his own existence he saw that two could be stronger than one. But he would never have June: he had nothing material to offer her, and she would not give up her children or the life she was used to. Things were better like this. It would be a long time before they tired of one another, and the lies June had to tell would come more readily with practice.

'My Ray would bring what you want,' said Mrs Brett.

She stood in Mrs Malmesbury's bedroom, her hair tied up in a cotton turban, arms crossed over her cerise nylon overall, and an expression of concern on her round face. On the days when she came, she took Mrs Malmesbury her breakfast in bed, a treat Mrs Malmesbury savoured. She would switch on the electric blanket and abandon herself to laziness while the Hoover whirred in the sitting-room. Then she had a bath, and dressed slowly while Mrs Brett cleaned the bedroom. She always enjoyed her bath on these mornings, for the fear of a possible fall was diminished by the presence of someone else in the flat. How very agreeable it would be if Mrs Brett came daily, instead of only twice a week.

Hitherto, Mrs Malmesbury had gone to the nearby shopping centre and bought her small wants in the supermarket. She had rather enjoyed it; by buying a little each day she never had much to carry, hampered as she was with her stick, and the outing filled up what would otherwise be empty hours. Her excursions with Ted covered other needs: clothes, when required, and the chemist. Since her accident, however – for that was how she described her collapse in the library – she had felt unsteady walking down the aisles of the big, brightly lit store. One day she'd felt slightly faint, and got frightened. It would be terrible to be taken ill in public again.

'I can buy my groceries when Mr Jessop takes me out in the car,' she said. She had not been out with Ted since her illness. 'He would carry them.'

'You could that,' agreed Mrs Brett. 'Extras, like. But you don't go out with him regular, now, do you? If I was to give my Ray your list, he could fetch them up for you every week. You could depend on it.'

'Crawley's do deliver here?'

'Twice a week, if wanted,' said Mrs Brett. 'Real, old-fashioned service, that's what they give.'

It seemed a good scheme. Mrs Brett's son must be a reliable young man.

'Very well, Mrs Brett. I'll get Mr Jessop to take me to Crawley's next Tuesday so that I can arrange for a monthly account. Then it will all be in order. And I'll telephone through every week with my list.'

She must remain in command of her own affairs. To surrender to Mrs Brett's kindly meant take-over offer would be to hasten her own inevitable decline. One must, at all costs, keep trying.

'How's the new book going?' Mr Vigors asked as he

pumped the chair down. He had just scaled Peter Guthrie's excellent teeth and filed a rough edge.

'Oh – much as usual,' said the writer.

'I haven't read it yet,' said Vigors. He had so far managed to give the impression of being an ardent Guthrie fan without ever reading a single one of his works. 'I expect you have to do a lot of research.' This was a safe assumption; authors usually did, Vigors was sure.

'Oh yes. I'm off to the library now, in fact,' said Guthrie. 'Checking up about Alamein – I was there, you know, but one forgets details. I'm starting a new series about a tank commander. There's a vogue for the last war just now.'

'So there is. It should be interesting,' said Vigors.

'I hope so,' said Guthrie. 'Well, I must be getting along.'

Nancy showed him out and ushered in the next patient. Then she went into the office, where Lorna was making out a list of supplies required from the surgical chemist.

'We've just had Peter Guthrie in, that writer,' she said. 'He's quite old. But he looks ever so distinguished. Quite a one, I should think he must have been, in his day.' Guthrie had given her what would have been described in one of his books as an ogle. 'You're a great reader, Lorna. Have you read any of his books? I haven't – they're too full of battles for me.'

'No, I haven't,' said Lorna. She tried to sound friendly, but the words came out in a snap.

Nancy, whose merchant seaman boy-friend was due home in a few days, was feeling benevolent and did not allow the curt answer to put her off. Poor old Lorna, she was all right really; just never got any fun. Too stiff, she was. She never minded staying late if Nancy was in a hurry to leave.

'Tell you what, Lorna. Joe'll be home over the

weekend. If I get him to bring a friend along, how'd you like to make up a four on Saturday night? We might go to the pictures and have a meal out.'

She and Joe always had a good time when he got home from a trip; he'd have money saved, and they'd eat a good meal, thinking all the while of what was to follow. Poor old Lorna missed all that. Maybe she just needed a bit of a push.

'No, thanks. Sorry – I can't,' said Lorna abruptly.

Nancy shrugged.

'Suit yourself,' she said.

Something twisted inside Lorna, some new emotion.

'I mean – it's nice of you. Nancy, thank you. But I can't,' she said, looking disturbed.

'Never mind. Another time,' Nancy said. She regarded the other girl in a bewildered way. It was the first time Nancy had seen her lose her composure.

The bell rang impatiently. Nancy should not have deserted Mr Vigors, alone with his patient, for so long.

'Oh, help!' she said, and left.

Lorna sat back when she had gone.

'I couldn't accept,' she thought forlornly. She would not have known what to say to Joe's friend – or to Joe – or even to Nancy. But she would be alone on Saturday evening. It would be pointless to come back to the surgery, for The Lindens would be in darkness and there would be nothing for her to watch. She could only sit there, imagining.

She went to the library that evening. Cecil was not there, but two of Peter Guthrie's novels were, and she took them home with her.

'Yes, Mum. All right. If you say so,' said Ray.

'A very old lady,' repeated his mother. 'Special attention, that's what she needs.'

'Right, Mum, I heard you.'

Would she never give over? She'd been nagging on about this old dame where she did her cleaning ever since he got back from the shop. Something about a weekly order and how he must deliver it.

'And it's no good just handing it to her. You must take it right into the kitchen, Ray,' his mother instructed. 'Poor old thing, she couldn't stoop down to lift it if you was to leave it outside. Still, she doesn't get out much. She'd always be there, when you called. I've my key, of course.'

For the first time in the conversation, Ray paid attention.

His mother had a key to some old girl's flat, and he would soon be visiting it on legitimate business. He'd have a look around. There might be things there worth nicking. He could easily borrow his mother's key without her noticing, and get another one cut.

Lorna was bicycling back from the library. The books by Peter Guthrie were in her bicycle basket, and her mind was in a tumult. That wicked June Titmuss, she kept thinking. She knew her first name, for she had long ago looked it up on the voter's list. How evil she was, and how ungrateful, when she had Cecil and those two children. She deserved the most terrible fate that could be devised, but what hurt her would also hurt Cecil.

What would he do, if he knew about her and Ted Jessop?

Lorna pedalled along. She brooded over the problem all the time now. The weather was fine and dry; most people had gone home from work but had not yet embarked on their evening's excursions, and the traffic was not heavy. She turned down Bridge Street, where the post office was, and the branch of the Midland Bank which Mr Vigors used, and rode silently along. Suddenly a man stepped from the kerb and rushed across the street in front of her. She swerved violently, braking hard, and almost fell as she avoided him. He had a most peculiar face, sort of squashed. He ran on over the road, between two cars, and along the pavement on the other side, but Lorna was too busy picking herself up to notice where he went after that. The books had flown out of her basket and fallen into the road. She picked them up and rubbed them with the sleeve of her coat. Only then did she become aware of cries coming from a figure, huddled on the pavement a short way ahead of her. She approached, and saw an elderly man struggling to his feet.

'Did you see him? Which way did he go?' It was Mr Beauchamp, the proprietor of Tansy's Tea Shoppe.

'What?' Lorna pushed her bike towards him. 'What's wrong? Are you ill?' For Mr Beauchamp was rubbing his head and looked very upset.

'That man – he ran right past you! He's robbed me,' cried Mr Beauchamp. 'Get the police, girl! Call the police!'

Mr Beauchamp was made of sterner stuff than Ray's first victim. The hook round his ankle had brought him down, but he'd hung on to the money-bag. Ray had had to kick him in the stomach to make him let go of the bag. But that girl on the bicycle had nearly knocked Ray over in his turn; he'd never heard her coming. Luckily he'd got the stocking over his face; she wouldn't be able to recognize him. Next time he'd work it differently: follow the victim from her place of work and rob her on the way, not just outside the bank; for it was the woman from Floradora's whom he planned to waylay next.

He drove the Imp back to the deserted building site where he kept it and broke open the bag with a screwdriver. It held a fat wad of notes and two bags of coins. He was wearing a padded anorak, and he stuffed the notes into a zipped pocket. Some of the coins went into another pocket, and the rest he left in the bag, which he stuffed under the seat of the car; they were too bulky to carry on him. Then he walked down the road to the nearest bus-stop and caught a bus into town, where he went to the cinema.

He sat back enjoying the film, which was a send-up of a western, feeling very pleased with himself and rather regretting that he could not round off the evening in the usual way with Brenda.

'And you didn't get a good look at the man at all, Miss Gibson?'

Lorna was at Felsbury Central Police Station. She had dialled 999 from the telephone box nearest to the bank and then returned to Mr Beauchamp, who was by now the centre of a small, exclaiming crowd. She was tempted to go away and leave him to it, but she had given her name over the telephone, so she supposed she was obliged to remain. The police arrived very quickly, so that she was only briefly exposed to the curiosity of the spectators, who realized that she had seen Mr Beauchamp's assailant. Now she was sitting opposite Detective Chief Inspector Purdy in his office, and a sergeant was making notes of all that she said.

'No. He came right in front of me. I nearly hit him with my bicycle,' said Lorna.

'Was he a big man?'

'Not really – sort of ordinary,' said Lorna, and then, seeing the frustration on the policeman's face, added, in an attempt at helpfulness, 'He was wearing an anorak. He wasn't as big as you.'

Purdy, who was six foot two, sighed. Few were, he found.

'Hair colour?' he tried.

'He was wearing a cap.' Lorna was certain of this. 'One of those peaked ones, cotton, aren't they? Dark. His face was odd – sort of flattish.'

'Perhaps he was wearing a mask? A stocking over his face?'

'Oh!' Light dawned. 'Yes – yes, he could have been.'

'It would distort his features. You've seen faces like that on television, perhaps?' Purdy suggested.

But Lorna had almost never watched television.

They let her go, after she had read and signed her statement. A policeman took her home in a van, with her bike in the back. Mr Beauchamp was all right, just shaken, and very, very angry. He had been taken to hospital but allowed to go home.

'We've got a bad one here,' Purdy said to his sergeant. 'It could be the same joker who got that publican a month ago. We never got a smell of who that could have been.'

'Funny girl, that,' said the sergeant. 'Fancy not watching telly.'

'Very refreshing,' said Purdy.

Chapter 8

Cecil must be told about June, Lorna had decided.

She tried printing sentences in black felt pen, using her left hand, and she tried cutting words out of a newspaper and pasting them on to sheets of plain paper. But she could not compose a message that satisfied her. WHERE WAS YOUR WIFE ON TUESDAY NIGHT? Or LOOK IN DUNSTABLE MEWS FOR YOUR WIFE ON TUESDAY were too cool. YOUR WIFE IS AN ADULTERESS was too sensational. In the end she bundled her efforts into a drawer till she could think of a better text.

Her part in Mr Beauchamp's unpleasant adventure was soon public knowledge, for the attack on him was described in the *Felsbury Gazette*. A reporter had interviewed her, a difficult job since she seemed to have nothing to say – but he had got some sort of a story out of her, and the paper had sent a photographer round too, who took a shot of her standing outside the paint shop.

'Not very like you, that photo, was it?' Nancy said. 'Weren't you scared?'

'No. Why should I have been? It was all over before I realized what had happened,' said Lorna.

Trust Lorna not to have other people's reactions, thought Nancy.

'Poor old Beauchamp. He's a nice old thing,' she said. 'Sure you won't change your mind about Saturday and come with us?'

'No, thanks.'

Next Saturday was one of Mr Vigors' working days, and it was Nancy's turn to be on duty with him. He never expected both girls to be there on a Saturday. It struck Lorna that Nancy might like the morning off, since she had a date. She said so, and offered to come in her place.

'Oh, would you, Lorna? Thanks! I did want to pop into La Boutique,' said Nancy. 'I'll do the same for you one day.'

But she would never be asked. Lorna never wanted extra free time.

It was a busy Saturday. Mr Vigors worked fast and Lorna kept him supplied with hypodermics and fillings. The last patient left at twelve-thirty, and Vigors himself was ready to go before she had finished clearing up.

'You'll lock up, Lorna?' he said.

'Yes.'

'Right, then. See you on Monday.'

He hurried back to his Susan, and Lorna relaxed. She filed away the morning's charts, and made sure that the tray by the chair and the bowl were gleaming, and the instruments all in the sterilizer. Then she looked out of the office window at The Lindens. They'd be starting their lunch, she thought. Or they might have gone out for the day. She could see no sign of any activity. She wouldn't wait now – it would be better to come back at dusk, when the lights were on.

She let herelf out of the house and walked towards the bus-stop. She always came to work on the bus; the girl who bicycled about the place with her hair in a pony-tail was a different being from the neat receptionist in her plastic raincoat and wool cap pulled over her coiled hair. She had got very wet riding to work on her bicycle in bad weather, so she had given it up. Sometimes, too, she rode round the town on the bus just for the company of other passengers; you might be lonely, but you were not alone on a bus.

Lorna walked round the corner and saw Cecil, with the two children, coming towards her. The little girl clung to his arm, and the boy was dragging back, looking at something behind him.

Somehow or other Lorna's legs kept on moving automatically, carrying her to their inevitable encounter. Would he recognize her? Should she speak?

Cecil had seen a pedestrian approaching, and he drew the children to one side of the pavement out of her way. As he did so, Lorna noticed a small object drop on the path ahead of her, and simultaneously Barty gave a shriek.

Lorna went forward and picked up the object, which was a toy car, and at the same moment the little boy escaped from his father's grasp and pounded towards her. She turned, still crouching, and held the car out towards him; Barty rushed headlong at her and in a moment her free arm was round him, holding his sturdy little body, while he took the car. His thick brown hair, soft and straight, brushed her face.

'Your car's quite safe,' said Lorna. 'Here, take it.'

Barty grabbed it and held it close to his chest. He looked at her mistrustfully.

'Say thank-you, Barty,' said Cecil's voice.

His trouser-legs appeared opposite Lorna's nose; she stayed motionless, still holding the little boy.

'And don't,' Cecil went on severely, 'ever rush off like that again. You might have run into the road, you weren't looking where you were going.'

Lorna stood up slowly. She was taller than Cecil; she had noticed it before, in the library and at the hospital.

'Why,' said Cecil, 'it's Miss –'

But her name would not come.

'Lorna Gibson,' she said eagerly. 'I work round the corner –'

'I know,' he cut in, remembering. 'The dentist's, isn't it? Well, thank you for rescuing Barty's car.'

'Not at all,' Lorna said, and stood there watching as the family trooped in through the gate of The Lindens. She could still feel the touch of Barty's firm little body.

Chapter 9

Each evening for a week Ray waited near Floradora's hoping to see Joyce Watson set off for the bank, but she never went there. By hurrying to lock the van up in the garage behind Crawley's, he was able to get round the corner and be lurking in the shadows as she closed up the shop. She would take some flowers out of the window and into the back of the shop, and pull others into position to make a display overnight. When at last she left, she caught a bus and travelled out to a new bungalow in the suburbs. Ray followed her there; she was easy to see, with her bright blonde hair, chic in her camel coat and patent shoes. He, in jeans, and jacket, might have been any young man, sitting at the other end of the bus; she never even glanced at him.

Perhaps she took the money home. But he had seen her at the bank, one Saturday.

Once again, at the weekend, she used the night safe. But Ray had no opportunity to intercept her for there were too many people about, and as she reached the bank he saw a police car cruising by.

He was impatient, now, to escape from Felsbury. Winter was coming; the flat seemed crowded whenever he was at home, for his brothers were growing, and as they got older they were becoming more demanding. There was more to life than driving a grocery van around a provincial town and spending the evening in a cramped, shabby flat with a couple of noisy kids and his uncommunicative mother and father. One Sunday he took thirty pounds from his hoard and went up to London in the Imp. He picked up a thin, bony bird who taught him a few things he didn't know before and disposed of any lingering regrets he might have about Brenda. She made him more eager than ever to break away.

Lorna had just put the kettle on and was buttering a piece of bread when her doorbell rang. The sound was so unusual that she jumped with surprise; her only callers were flag-sellers.

She went downstairs and opened the door cautiously, keeping it on the chain. A tall man in a raincoat stood outside.

'Detective Chief Inspector Purdy, Miss Gibson,' he said. 'Could I have a word?'

'Oh! Yes, I suppose so. You'd better come in,' she said and opened the door.

Purdy came into the narrow hallway and Lorna retreated to the lowest stair; there was not enough space for both of them between the door and the bottom tread. Her bicycle occupied the area at the side. It was clean and well-kept, he noticed; the chrome shone, and a padlock and chain secured the rear wheel. He stepped forward, and Lorna retreated up another step. She realized that he meant her to ask him up to her room.

She turned. 'This way, please,' she said, as she would have instructed a patient at the surgery.

'Lived here long, have you?' Purdy asked chattily as he followed her up the stairs.

'Three years.'

'What a nice room!'

It was a surprise. With the lamp on, though it was not yet dark outside, the vivid reds and oranges and purples glowed.

'I was making some tea. Would you like a cup?' she said stiffly.

'Thanks very much,' said Purdy.

Lorna made tea by pouring the water into a mug in which a tea-bag already reposed; she owned no teapot. She made the Chief Inspector's tea in a similar manner, dunking the bag and stirring it round before fishing it out with a spoon. She had had to wash the second mug; it was dusty with disuse.

'Oh – sugar, sorry. I forgot,' she said, and vanished again through her curtain. She did not take it herself, and bought very little. There was some in a screwed-up packet; she tipped it into an egg-cup and produced a teaspoon. Purdy drank the tea with the spoon in the mug, biffing his nose; he did not know what to do with it otherwise.

'That man who attacked Mr Beauchamp. Have you remembered anything else about him?' he asked.

'No.'

'You're our only hope, you know,' said Purdy. 'I thought something more might have come back to you.'

'It hasn't.'

What a defeating sort of girl. She was no help at all. Yet there must have been something, if only she could be persuaded to remember it. Meanwhile they stood, with their mugs in their hands, occupying most of the floor space in Lorna's room. It was not very cosy.

Lorna, though tall, found the policeman's bulk overwhelming; he was too close.

'Won't you sit down,' she said, waving vaguely at the armchair, and she withdrew to the divan, where she perched on the edge furthest away from him.

Purdy sat down and waited for her to say something else.

It was very peculiar, having a visitor. Of course, this was no social call, so there was no need to worry about being unable to think of something to talk about.

'He wore a dark anorak, but I told you that. And about the hat,' said Lorna. 'He moved quickly. I suppose he was young. I forgot all about him as soon as I saw Mr Beauchamp on the ground.'

It was the longest speech Purdy had heard her make.

'Very natural,' he said, drinking some tea. He lodged the teaspoon near the handle with a finger. He'd swear the girl was scared almost out of her wits. Probably expecting her boyfriend round and afraid he'd get the wrong idea. It was a faint hope, coming here at all. They had watched all the banks ever since the incident and seen no one loitering suspiciously.

'Been to Spain?' he asked, indicating the posters.

'Majorca. Some time ago now.'

'Very nice, I expect.'

'Yes.' Lorna did not enlarge. 'More tea?'

'No, thanks. I must be going. Sorry to take up your time on a Saturday. I expect you're going out.'

'Yes.'

Purdy stood up and Lorna took his mug. As he turned to go he noticed the wastepaper basket full of crumpled newspaper. He could see a page with spaces where small parts had been cut out.

'Well, I won't keep you any longer. You'll let us know if you think of anything?'

'Yes.'

'Don't trouble to come down. I'll let myself out,' said Purdy.

But she did, and although she was soon going out herself, she put up the chain.

Ray arrived with the groceries just before Ted was due to collect Mrs Malmesbury. Travelling up in the lift, he set the box down and slicked back his hair so that he would look neat and dependable before ringing the bell.

'Crawley's order,' he said when the old lady opened the door.

'Ah – you're Mrs Brett's boy?'

Mrs Malmesbury saw a pale lad, with light blue eyes and straight brown hair, very ordinary in appearance. He seemed helpful.

'That's right. I'll just carry it through, shall I?' said Ray, stepping into the flat.

'Thank you – in the kitchen, through there, if you would,' said Mrs Malmesbury.

Ray walked on with the box, looking around him as he went. This was a bit of all right: fitted carpets, sofa and chairs covered in some sort of flowered stuff, a shelf full of books on one side of the fireplace and ornaments on the other, including some silver. His interest sharpened, but it wouldn't do to seem too noticing.

'The order's all complete,' he said, 'I checked it myself.' This was untrue, but the assistants were reliable.

'That's good of you. Here.' Mrs Malmesbury fumbled in her purse. She took out a tenpenny piece and gave it to him.

'Oh, ta!'

'Another time you must have a cup of tea, after bringing the box all this way, but I'm going out soon. I go out most Tuesdays,' Mrs Malmesbury volunteered.

Ray tucked the information away. It might come in handy.

Ted drew up behind the grocer's van. He saw Ray come out of the flats, get into it and drive away, but he was preoccupied, listening to the Humber's engine: it was running too fast. Mrs Malmesbury wasn't going shopping; they'd made a minor excursion the week before to arrange about Crawley's, but she'd felt very tired after that and had gone straight home. Today he was taking her to have lunch with Hesther and Edgar Ford.

'How are you feeling?' he asked, settling her into the car. He wrapped a rug around her knees and Mrs Malmesbury sighed with pleasure. It was delightful to be cosseted.

'Much better, thank you,' she said, but admitted, 'A little wobbly still.'

'Straight to Diddington, then?'

'Could we go to the library on the way? I've got two books that are due for return, and someone may be wanting them. But I wonder if you would mind changing them for me? I don't think I'm quite up to it myself, yet.'

'I'll be glad to,' said Ted. 'But what shall I get for you?'

'Oh, that nice Mr Titmuss will find me something,' said Mrs Malmesbury. 'Just ask for him. Do you know, he came out to the hospital twice, bringing me books I'd asked for? Now, wasn't that kind?'

'Very,' said Ted. He felt a shock at hearing Cecil's name uttered aloud. Somehow, he successfully managed never to think of him; when June and he were together, she took all his attention, and when they were parted he resumed his own life, which meant work and little else. If his thoughts wandered in June's direction, he pictured her in Floradora's.

He parked at a meter near the library, and took off his cap, leaving it on the car seat.

'I'll be as quick as I can,' he said.

'I'm quite warm and comfortable,' Mrs Malmesbury assured him. She closed her eyes when he had gone. A little nap would just set her up before she met Hester.

Miss Binks was on duty at the desk. Ted told her the books were from Mrs Malmesbury and asked that Mr Titmuss should choose her two more.

'Oh, but I can't possibly ask Mr Titmuss to attend to you,' exclaimed Miss Binks in horror. 'He looked after Mrs Malmesbury before, I know, but he happened to be standing nearby when she was taken ill.'

You'd think the fellow was God, the way she spoke about him.

'Which is he?' snapped Ted.

'He's in there.' Miss Binks lowered her voice and pointed to the glass partition. 'In the office. Talking to the head librarian.'

Through the parted slats of the venetian blinds, Ted could see two men: one was tall, with grey hair, and the other shorter, going bald. He recognized the shorter one; he had been in the little procession following Mrs Malmesbury's stretcher that day.

'The shorter one?'

'Yes.' Miss Binks's voice was hushed, as if the two could overhear. 'I will find something suitable for Mrs Malmesbury,' she said, and swam importantly off towards the shelves.

Well, that should be all right. While he waited for her, Ted watched Cecil. So that was June's husband. He looked harmless. Unconsciously, Ted stretched, standing to his own full height. The two men were moving now: still talking, they came into the main library and passed close to Ted. Cecil was not really a small man, but he was not tall, and he was slightly built. The bald spot on his head was quite pronounced; he looked very ordinary. What would he think if he knew his wife's lover was standing ten feet from him?

Ted felt no guilt. It happened all the time. As long as Cecil never found out, it wouldn't hurt him. After all, it was his fault. Obviously, he didn't have the knack.

Chapter 10

After the surgery closed on Tuesday, Lorna did not leave. She had made a desperate plan. She turned off the lights, closed all the doors, and camped on the landing with a candle, so that no chink of light could betray her presence. She'd brought extra sandwiches, and she could use the office kettle to make tea. She passed the time until June left, ostensibly for her Italian lesson, by reading one of Peter Guthrie's books. It revealed interesting facts about weapons at. Malplaquet; the hero was involved in a flirtation with a married woman whose husband seemed to be a sadist, and simultaneously with a young girl of great innocence; even to Lorna, his dealings with both seemed to indicate scant feeling for either. They appeared to serve merely as props to the hero's vanity. The sadistic husband was killed in battle, and the hero tried to seduce the widow; he tried also to seduce the young girl. In both cases virtue triumphed, leaving the hero bitter.

At seven-fifteen Lorna blew out her candle, hid the traces of her stay, and let herself out of the house. A few minutes later she rang the bell at The Lindens.

Cecil answered. He wore a shapeless fawn cardigan and he looked tired.

'Oh – Miss Er,' he said, blinking at her in surprise. He still could not remember her name.

'Mr Titmuss, I'm sorry to disturb you. I came to see your wife,' said Lorna, her voice firm despite her pounding heart.

'She's out, I'm afraid. Can I give her a message?' said Cecil, looking perplexed. Did June know this girl? A gust of cold wind caught at them both as they stood there, and he added, 'It's cold – come in, won't you?'

It was so easy. She was through the door. She tried not to stare, but caught a swift impression of yellow-patterned wallpaper and white paint: the house had been transformed.

'I'm collecting for a jumble sale. For Tibetans,' said Lorna. She'd got the idea after seeing a picture of the Dalai Lama: it was sufficiently unusual not to clash with any other cause; she needed only a pretext.

'Tibetans? Well – I expect my wife could find something. I'll ask her. Will you call back?' said Cecil.

'Who is it, Daddy?' came a voice. A small figure in blue pyjamas appeared at the top of the stairs: Barty.

'Barty, go back to bed,' said Cecil.

'Hullo,' said Lorna. 'How's your green car?'

'It's lost a wheel,' said Barty. 'I'll show you.' He vanished, and there was a clatter overhead. Cecil gave Lorna a rueful glance.

'I shouldn't have asked,' she said.

'It was nice of you to remember.'

As if she could forget.

Barty reappeared with the car, and brought it downstairs for her inspection. Sure enough, a wheel was missing.

'Oh dear,' said Lorna. 'I expect you'll find it tomorrow. Now you'd better go back to bed.'

Like a lamb, Barty obeyed. When he reached the top of the stairs he turned and said, 'Come and tuck me up,' addressing the command to Lorna.

'Now Barty,' Cecil began, but Lorna interrupted.

'May I?' she asked eagerly.

'Well – yes, if you don't mind,' said Cecil, astonished. Mind? She could not wait!

Barty's room was painted pale primrose; curtains patterned with soldiers were drawn across the windows. His small bed was close to the wall, and a battered giraffe lay on his pillow. Lorna bent and tucked him in as if she had done it every night of his life. She received in return a warm, wet kiss. Cecil, who had followed her upstairs, witnessed this interlude from the door, and Janet, who had overheard it all, now called from her room.

'Go to sleep,' said Cecil, opening her door. 'It's just Miss Gibson collecting things for a sale.' Her name had come back to him.

'I want to see,' said Janet, with determination.

'Perhaps you'd just say good night?' Cecil said.

Lorna put her head round the door. Two bright eyes glittered at her in darkness that was broken only by the light from the landing.

'Goodnight,' said Lorna.

'Goodnight,' said Janet, in an affected high, piping voice.

'I'm sorry about all that,' said Cecil, as he stood aside for Lorna to go downstairs ahead of him.

'It was my fault for disturbing you,' said Lorna, and then, 'Oh, how lovely!' She had seen the model of Wells Cathedral on the window-sill.

Cecil looked pleased.

'It's made from matches, isn't it? Did you do it?' As if she didn't know.

'Yes. I'm making Notre Dame at the moment,' said Cecil. 'Would you like to see it?'

'Please.'

So she went into the room which she had seen so often already. There was the table; there, on the wall, was the plan of Notre Dame; the glue, the tweezers, and a pile of matches were at hand.

'How wonderful! How much longer will it take you?' She studied the model.

'Oh – several months. Perhaps a year. It's slow work,' said Cecil. 'I do a little nearly every evening.'

She knew he did.

'We don't go out a lot. Reliable baby-sitters aren't easy to find. So my wife and I each have our hobby,' said Cecil. 'My wife is learning Italian. She's at her class tonight.'

Supposing she said, 'Oh no, she's not! You'll find her in Dunstable Mews.' What would he say?

Lorna took a deep breath.

'I would baby-sit, if you wanted to go out together,' she said.

'Would you?' He looked at her in amazement.

'I'd like to.'

She must be reliable, holding the job that she did. Besides, you had only to look at her.

'Please don't hesitate,' she said. She mustn't seem too keen. 'You could telephone me at Mr Vigors' surgery.'

'That's very kind of you. I'll tell my wife. We might be very thankful to take you up on that offer,' he said.

'I mean it,' said Lorna.

'Yes,' said Cecil. 'I can see that you do.'

He showed her to the door.

'I'll remember the Tibetans. June will find them something,' he promised, and let her out of the house, into the night.

Lorna had gone to work by bus, as usual, that morning, and now returned the same way. She passed the journey in a daze, re-living every moment of her adventure. As she walked home from the bus-stop a figure came out of a side-street in front of her; it was a young man in jeans, and an anorak. He wore a peaked cap. Despite her preoccupation, Lorna noticed him. They walked on, one behind the other, passing La Boutique, Tansy's Tea Shoppe, and Floradora's. At the flower shop the young man stopped;

96

he looked in the window, and then, hearing Lorna, who was wearing leather boots, not her usual rubber-soled shoes, approaching, he looked round. She saw his face for a moment, pale, with very light blue eyes. Then he turned from her and ran across the road. In that moment he gave himself away, for she was reminded at once of Mr Beauchamp's attacker who had fled in front of her bicycle.

Ted had enjoyed the outing to Diddington with Mrs Malmesbury. Sitting in The Rose and Crown, being paid to while away the time over a ploughman's lunch, was an easy way of making money. When he fetched her at half-past two, though, she looked tired; the trip had been a strain.

'General Ford is a very old man,' she said as they drove back towards the town.

'Yes.' It could not be denied.

'Once he was so handsome. And brave. He won the D.S.O. and bar.'

'Is that so?'

'Yes.'

She fell silent, and in the mirror he saw her blinking, as if she was on the verge of tears. It must be sad to see your friends becoming physical wrecks. After a while he glanced at her again, and saw that she had fallen asleep.

While he was in the pub, Peter Guthrie had come in. It seemed he was a regular. He remembered Ted, and told him that he had made a start on the first book in his new tank commander series.

'Should make good reading,' said Ted. 'Does he go for the birds?'

'Well, yes,' said Guthrie. 'Women play quite a part in all my books.'

'That Gadsby of yours doesn't like them much,' said Ted.

'He does! He's always involved with some woman or other,' said Guthrie, amused at this criticism.

'Oh, he likes what they're for, to his way of thinking,' Ted allowed. 'But it's all one-way, isn't it? Gadsby's only thinking of himself and what he'll get out of it. He never thinks about the bird and what's in it for her.'

'Well – no, I suppose he doesn't,' said Guthrie. 'But does any man?'

'I hope so,' said Ted, really shocked. 'Don't you?'

Peter Guthrie, successful author, and respectable married father of three, stared at his challenger.

'Are you married?' he asked.

'No. But I've made plenty of birds happy,' said Ted calmly. 'Not like your Gadsby. But I suppose you've a reason for making him like that.'

Some years ago Guthrie's wife had suddenly fallen in love with their family solicitor, an older man than Guthrie, less well preserved. The experience had been a shattering one for all three of them; the solicitor, a widower, felt as deeply for Audrey as she for him. For some months the Guthries' marriage had been threatened; then Audrey returned to what Guthrie described as her right mind; she said goodbye to the solicitor, but maintained that it was only for the children's sake – they were all still at school at the time – that she had abandoned the affair.

'I don't know what you see in that chap,' Guthrie had said.

'It's what he sees in me,' Audrey had replied. 'And the tenderness.'

Guthrie had found the very word embarrassing. In the world where Gadsby moved, men were men; they took what they wanted and moved onwards, ever ready for the next opportunity. In real life, of course, it was harder to do that, for some conventions had to be observed, and occasion did not offer very often, but when it did there was no need to waste time on frills. To be soft was, Guthrie considered, to be cissy.

He was, though, unable to answer Ted.

Chapter 11

'If we went into it together, we'd be on to a good thing,' Charlie said to Ted. They were sitting in his workshop on two upturned boxes, drinking tea out of enamel mugs. Ted had no bookings that afternoon and had spent it helping Charlie strip down an old MG Magnette ready for fitting a new engine. 'There'd be room for the Humber. We could get a driver. We'd make a lot more money if you stayed in the workshop and we paid a bloke.'

'I like it on the road,' said Ted. He was always happy behind the wheel of his car, aware of the sweet purr of the engine, the power so swiftly increased by the touch of his foot, the fresh air beyond the warm cell of the car.

'Well, we could train a lad. Good mechanics are hard to find, as you well know. I'd never manage without you giving me a hand now and then. I tell you, Ted, we'd be on to a good thing. It's right near the by-pass; we'd get a lot of trade, and still be close to town to keep what we've got here.'

'You've got as much as you can handle here,' said Ted.

'I know, but if we'd more space we could branch into the used car trade. There's still money to be made with that.'

'Well, I'll think about it,' Ted said.

Charlie had heard of a business coming up for sale, a

garage with pumps and a bungalow as well as a workshop equipped with every aid to modernized servicing. It was a thriving concern already, and he could not raise enough money to go into it alone; besides, he could not manage it without a partner. He was sure that with Ted's co-operation it would be a worthwhile venture.

'There'd be room for you in the bungalow. Till you wanted a place of your own. Doreen'd be glad to have you.' Doreen was Charlie's wife.

Ted was not so sure about that. And what about June? He could not take her to Charlie's bungalow.

'When would it be?' he asked.

'Oh, not until well into the new year.'

Charlie would get a good price for his present place; it was behind an office block and ripe for redevelopment.

'Your lease runs out next year,' he reminded Ted.

'Yes.' He would have to make new plans then, and for this reason alone Charlie's proposition was worth considering.

He told June about it at their next meeting.

'Do you want to go in with him?' she asked.

'It could be a very good thing,' said Ted. 'Charlie's got a head for business. We get on all right. Doreen'd go on the pumps.'

'It sounds exciting,' said June. 'Shall I leave Cecil and come too? I could drive the taxi.'

He thought of her grinding the gears on his precious car.

'You'd hate it,' he said. 'Hanging about in all weathers. And you've your kids. You'd never leave them.'

No, she wouldn't; nor her comfortable house and improving status.

'I'm not giving you up,' she said.

'You will. You'll get tired of all this,' he said. 'The winter will make a difference.'

He knew, without putting the thought into words, that what would end their affair would be the same thing that had made it such a success: the fundamental contrast between Cecil and himself. She'd find someone else, someone more like herself, with more to offer her; or maybe she'd settle down and make the best of things with Cecil, perhaps have another kid, even.

The thought disturbed him, and as if she had shared it, June turned to him.

'I'll never get tired of this,' she said.

It was raining, so Nancy was having her lunch in the office. In winter, when it was too cold for the garden, she and Mr Carruthers usually sat in what had once been a conservatory, but staring at the rain was depressing.

'We had a smashing time on Saturday, Lorna. You should have come,' she said, biting into a chocolate eclair so that the cream splurged out. Lorna watched with distaste as her tongue flicked out like a cat's to lick it up. 'Joe's friend Norman is ever so nice.'

'Where did you go?' she asked, making an effort.

'To Giovanni's. We had a lovely meal. My sister came in the end, for Norman, but she's only a kid. You'd have been better,' said Nancy kindly. Lorna looked different today, less buttoned up. Something had happened to her. 'You got a boyfriend?' she asked.

Lorna shook her head.

'I'm not the type,' she said.

'Silly! Everyone's the type,' said Nancy. 'You'd look quite different if you wore your hair loose. Let's try it.' She put out a hand to touch the other girl's hair and Lorna jumped back as if she had been stung.

'Leave me alone! Don't touch me,' she cried.

'Oh – sorry, I'm sure,' said Nancy, her eager expression instantly snuffed out.

'I'm sorry, Nancy. I didn't mean to snap at you.' Lorna was contrite at once, and managed to show it. 'It's just that – oh, I don't know how to explain.'

'You don't like people touching you. Is that it?' said Nancy slowly, looking at Lorna speculatively. She was a good-hearted girl, reluctant to take offence where none was intended. 'I wonder if that's really it?'

'What do you mean?'

'Maybe you're really longing for it,' Nancy said.

Detective Chief Inspector Purdy had rung Lorna's bell and waited.

This time she was expecting him, and was ready. She ran quickly down the stairs and opened the door.

'Come up, please,' she said.

Her hair was uncoiled, tied back in a pony-tail; she wore a maroon sweater over dark slacks, and she looked much less remote than the tense girl he had interviewed before. Purdy was intrigued by the change.

The gas fire was lit, the curtains were drawn, and he could hear the kettle.

'You'll have some tea,' she said. She had remembered the sugar, and when she reappeared with the mugs on the tray it was in a small bowl which looked as if it might have started life as an ashtray. The problem of what to do with the spoon was not resolved, however. If Purdy took it out of the mug it might drip on the carpet.

'You've something to tell me,' he said.

'Yes. Not much.'

Lorna had telephoned the police station that evening, after spending most of the day wondering if she should tell the police about the man she had seen the night before. It was so vague. But there was poor Mr Beauchamp to be thought of; he was lucky not to have been really hurt. There might be another victim. And something had happened to her after that brief flare-up with Nancy; in fact things had been happening ever since she entered The Lindens: weird sensations she'd not known for years and had forgotten.

'I saw that man,' she said. 'At least, I think it was him.'

She had said as much to the constable who had taken the call. Purdy had been passing the desk at the time and had instantly said he would come round to see her.

'Where did you see him?' he asked.

Lorna explained, hoping the inspector would not ask where she had been.

He did not, but he asked the time.

'Soon after nine. He was walking up the road ahead of me. I didn't take any notice of him until he suddenly ran off.'

'Why did he do that?'

'I don't know. He'd been walking along looking in the shop windows. I had noticed that.'

'So you caught up with him?'

'Yes.'

She hadn't realized why the man had taken flight: for flight it must have been. Lorna's picture had been in the paper. Recognition had been mutual.

'You'd know him now if you saw him again?'

'Oh yes. I got a good look at him this time. But I couldn't be certain he was the one who attacked Mr Beauchamp,' Lorna said earnestly. 'It was just that the hat was the same, and he moved the same way.'

'I'd like you to come to the station with me,' said Purdy. 'To look at some photographs. Our rogues' gallery. You might pick him out. If not, we'll try to make up a picture of him from your description.'

'Now?'

'Yes. Don't worry about your bicycle. We'll bring you back home again afterwards.'

Chapter 12

'Tibetan refugees? But that's not a new thing,' said June.

'No. Deserving, however,' said Cecil.

'I expect I can find a few things,' said June. 'Will she come back for them?'

'Yes.' Cecil got up from the breakfast table. 'She said she'd sit in for us, any time.' He mouthed something over the children's heads as they tucked in to their Weetabix.

'The Red Cross Ball,' June interpreted.

They had been sent invitations to this annual event, sponsored by the mayor, which was a social achievement; the tickets were expensive, but it was an important occasion in Felsbury's year and they would have liked to go. However, the problem of finding someone who would not mind staying late with the children had not been solved and they were resigned to the impossibility of accepting.

Cecil went out of the kitchen to fetch his brief-case and June followed.

'You think this girl would be all right?' she asked.

'Oh, yes. She's a very sensible sort of girl. And she works for the dentist round the corner. You could telephone her there.'

'We'd be very late back,' said June.

'I could take her home afterwards. She can't live far from here.'

'Yes. Or she could stay the night.'

'Good idea. You arrange it, dear. Her name is Gibson. We'll send for the tickets as soon as you've fixed it up.'

'I'll need something to wear,' June tried.

'I expect we could manage that,' said Cecil, with a smile and went up to the bathroom.

June went back to the kitchen; it was a safe bet that he would agree to a new dress; he would want her to reflect credit on him. She urged the children on with their breakfast.

Cecil reappeared five minutes later smelling faintly of toothpaste. He kissed June on the cheek and received hugs from the children. Then he left for the library. The car started easily; he let it warm up while he cleaned the windscreen; odd that it had failed June that time – it had behaved perfectly ever since. Later, waiting for the traffic lights to change, he mused on the fact that you married because you wanted to share your life with a particular person; then you saw very little of them, for you shared more of your waking hours with those you worked among. You went home to eat, sleep, read the paper and follow your hobby; you could know less about how your family spent the day than about someone who meant nothing to you but who happened to share the office. He found it hard to imagine June's mornings at Floradora's. There must be more to it than wrapping up bunches of chrysanthemums and making funeral wreaths. And the children: off they went to school each day and were engulfed by another existence altogether. Barty still related most of his adventures, but Janet had friends who came to tea with her and giggled over secrets. Her world had enlarged and he could not follow her into it, though up to a point he could still protect her. He dreaded the day when this would no longer be possible. It was all so sad; no one could have a relationship with another person which touched at every point, however deeply committed; one could only make the most of every fleeting contact.

June telephoned him at the library during the afternoon.

Lorna had agreed to come on the night of the Red Cross Ball.

June's telephone call had startled Lorna. She took almost all the calls at the surgery; they were nearly always people wanting appointments, and she had never received a personal call before.

The woman's voice was low and pleasant.

'Miss Gibson? You called last night about Tibetan refugees? I'm June Titmuss.'

'Oh yes!' A gasp from Lorna.

'I'll find you some things. And my husband said you might consider baby-sitting for us. Is that right?'

'Quite right.'

It was all fixed up in a matter of minutes. Lorna panicked when offered a bed for the night and said she could easily cycle home, but June insisted that Cecil would drive her, so that was agreed. Lorna was left regretting that through her own folly she had lost the chance of spending a night under the same roof as Cecil; and June was relieved because this was an easier arrangement.

'Will a pound be all right?' June asked.

'Oh, I don't want any money,' said Lorna. 'It will be a pleasure to come.'

June laughed.

'Well, give it to the Tibetans, then,' she said, and rang off.

'She didn't recognize him among our customers,' said Detective Chief Inspector Purdy.

Chief Superintendent Whitchurch pushed his chair back, took off his glasses and rubbed his eyes.

'Sure she knew what she was talking about?'

'Yes.'

'Those cut-out bits of newspaper you saw. Any more of them about last night?'

Purdy had discreetly peered into Lorna's waste-paper basket the evening before.

'No. There was just the wrapper from a bar of chocolate,' he said. 'She's a funny sort of girl. Nervy – neurotic, maybe.'

'Well, we've had no complaints of anonymous letters,' said Whitchurch. 'She may have a passion for paper games. What are you doing about this man?' He indicated a photofit picture that had been composed with Lorna's help.

'I thought we'd pass it round quietly. Have a look-out kept, but no fuss. It might ring a bell with someone,' said Purdy.

'Do that,' said the superintendent. 'I hope the girl will keep her eyes open too.'

'Oh, I think she will,' said Purdy. 'She may be our best bet, cycling about as she does all over the place.'

Lorna's immediate reaction to June was that she sounded so nice. The voice on the telephone had been warm and friendly. How deceptive outward appearances could be.

She decided to go for the Tibetan hand-outs on Saturday afternoon, when there was a good chance that Cecil would be there, although she knew he worked some Saturdays.

It was a clear, cold day, but by the time Lorna had summoned the courage to ring the bell dusk was falling.

Janet, wearing a large apron, opened the door, and Cecil appeared almost at once, saying, 'Who is it, pet?' in an abstracted manner. Then he saw for himself.

'Ah – Miss Gibson. You've come for the jumble.'

'If it's convenient.'

'Of course. Come in, do. You must excuse us, we're all in a mess,' said Cecil. He too wore an apron, and now Barty appeared with a tea-towel tied round him.

'It's Mummy's birthday tomorrow, and we're icing her cake,' said Janet.

'My wife's out,' said Cecil. 'So we're seizing our chance.'

'It's a surprise,' said Barty. 'Come and see.'

He put out a sticky hand and led Lorna off to the kitchen, where on the table stood a large cake covered in thick white icing. *Happy Birthday* was written in shaky pink letters on the top, and blobs of pink adorned the base. Janet picked up the icing bag, knelt on a chair, and bent over the cake.

'Now *Mummy*,' she said, and squeezed some more icing out to finish the legend she was inscribing.

'What a lovely cake,' said Lorna. She felt tears pricking her eyes: all this love, this cake being made by a devoted trio, for someone who did not deserve it. Cecil stood behind the scribe watching intently as she laboriously wrote a spidery M; he held a knife, and adroitly cut short the trail of icing when the letter was complete.

'Now up a bit, for the U,' he instructed, and added to Lorna, 'I'm so sorry to keep you. I'll get the things in a minute.'

'It's all right. I'm not in a hurry,' said Lorna. The icing would harden if they left it; it was so long since she had seen a cake being iced that she was surprised she could remember how it was done at all.

'Mummy's gone to a wedding,' said Barty. He had taken a spoon from a drawer and was finishing off the remains of white icing left in a bowl.

Janet squeezed on, her tongue protruding. Her audience watched, motionless, as she finished the Y with a flourish.

'Now kisses,' commanded Barty. 'Put twenty-nine kisses.'

110

'There isn't room for twenty-nine,' said Cecil. 'Let's put three. One each.'

They did, Barty putting the biggest and getting icing all over his fingers. He already had a sugar beard and moustache.

'Barty, you've as much icing on your face as there is on the cake,' Cecil said, laughing at him.

'It's a lovely cake,' said Lorna fervently. 'When did you bake it?'

'First thing this morning. We began as soon as Mummy went out, didn't we?' Cecil appealed to his helpers. 'So it's a bit soft to hold the icing. My wife works at Floradora's,' he added. 'They've got a big wedding today, at Diddington. June did the flowers in the church and the bride's bouquet, and she's over there now. I'll just get you the things – I'll have to wash first.'

He, too, was sticky. His face was flushed and he had a speck of icing attached to his wispy brown hair; Lorna had an urge to pick it out for him. Cecil ran water into the sink and soaped his hands and bare forearms; there were fine fair hairs on them, she saw.

'I'm finishing this bowl, Daddy,' said Janet, who was busy now spooning up the pink icing.

'All right. We'll wash up in a minute.'

'Mummy won't be back for ages,' Janet said.

'We don't know when she'll be back,' said Cecil. 'You two go up and clean your teeth, as soon as you've finished guzzling that sugar. Now, Miss Gibson.'

He went out of the kitchen, and Lorna followed slowly, reluctant to leave the intimate scene.

'It's bad for the children to eat all that icing, but it's only once a year,' he said. 'Now, here we are.' He opened a drawer in a chest in the hall and took out a green plastic Marks and Spencer's carrier.

'You have made the house nice,' Lorna said, looking round. 'I knew it before you bought it.'

'Oh – did you? Yes, we've worked hard on it. White paint makes a lot of difference,' said Cecil.

Lorna took the carrier from him.

'Please thank your wife for these,' she said.

'That's all right,' said Cecil. 'Thank you, for saying you'll baby-sit.'

'I'm looking forward to it,' said Lorna truthfully.

She rode swiftly home on her bicycle, and hurried up to her room, where she unpacked the bag. There was a small pair of blue cotton shorts, a threadbare yellow tee-shirt and a minute pair of white tights. And, much darned, a man's sleeveless pullover, in beige. All were spotless, as the house had been. June not only owned a pleasant voice but was also a good housewife.

It would all have been simpler if she were not.

Ted was driving the bride to the church, and the bride and groom to the reception; it added a fillip to June's day. They were to meet afterwards, as soon as both could get away.

The day before, she had arranged the flowers in the church and at the bride's house, helped by Tracey from the shop.

The children had gone home from school with a friend and June had collected them later.

Today, Cecil had let her bring the car when she came over with the bouquets. She was independent.

She sat at the back of the church and thought about Ted, outside with the Humber. So near, yet remote; earlier, when she passed him, he had remained impassive, not even smiling.

'It's the bride's day,' he'd told her already. 'She's paid for me. I can't give her less than my full attention.'

As he gave it to her at appropriate times, thought June, with anticipation. She watched him holding the car door open, while bride and groom climbed in after the photographs had been taken. It was cold; there had been jokes about the bride shivering. Ted's thick, springy hair was visible beneath his uniform cap; June imagined the feel of it under her hand. There was excitement in being together in a public place like this, their intimate knowledge a secret.

'You did the flowers, didn't you?' said a woman at the reception; she was about fifty, faded-looking, with tired brown eyes in a pale, lined face. 'They're lovely.'

'Oh, thank you!' June was glad that someone had spoken to her, for she knew no one except the bride and her family. She remembered Joyce's instructions. 'I'm with Floradora's, from Felsbury,' she added.

'I'll remember,' said the woman. 'I've got a daughter who might want to get married one day.'

'Not yet, I hope,' said the man who was with her. He was tall and looked distinguished, though he was getting on a bit, thought June. He was regarding her with interest.

'I'll give you a card,' she said, and took one of Floradora's business cards from her bag.

'Put your name on it,' said the man.

June wrote it on the back. She held the card out to the woman, but the man took it.

'Do you live in Diddington?' she asked.

'Yes,' said the man. 'My name is Peter Guthrie.'

He waited expectantly, as if she should have heard of it, but June had not. 'And this is my wife,' he added, turning to find her at his elbow. But Mrs Guthrie had moved away; she was talking to a very old man with a face like a tortoise, who was bent almost double.

'Where's she got to? Oh, there she is, talking to old General Ford. He's nearly a hundred, my dear. Would you believe it?'

Easily, thought June, but she opened her eyes very wide and said, 'No, really?'

'Past it by now, poor fellow,' said Guthrie. He was irked that June had not recognized his name and he wanted to impress her; he could not address her by her own name yet, for he could not read the card without his glasses and he did not want to reveal this weakness to her by putting them on.

'Let me get you some more champagne,' he said, and stopped a passing waiter. 'Tell me, what else do you do besides arrange flowers exquisitely?'

When June finally reached Dunstable Mews, Ted had been waiting for twenty minutes and they had their first row.

'You in there with all the nobs,' he said bitterly. 'You'll chuck me for one of them yet.'

'Oh Ted, I won't,' she said. 'Never.' And after a time, 'I believe you're jealous. How lovely.'

But she might.

Chapter 13

Mrs Malmesbury put the telephone down, and began to cry again.

Edgar was dead. Old Edgar Ford, once her love. He had died in his sleep, quite suddenly, on Saturday night, after a happy afternoon spent at a wedding.

A sleep and a forgetting, she said to herself. But she did not like to think of the forgetting part.

Hesther was bearing up well; her daughter had arrived from Yorkshire; her son was on his way from Brussels. She, Mrs Malmesbury, was not needed; nor, indeed, would she have been any help; she was too fragile.

'I'm no use to anyone,' she said, and angrily poked her stick at a harmless chair.

She had just telephoned Ted to change their arrangement for Tuesday: instead of a shopping trip she now needed him the next day, Wednesday, to take her to Edgar's funeral. Ted had been very understanding; to her great relief he was able to make the change.

She was still weeping when Ray arrived with the grocery order. He came twice a week now, with small amounts. It was his own idea, in case she forgot something the first time. She looked forward to his visits and had told his mother what a nice boy he was.

He was shocked when she opened the door to him with a face ravaged by tears. He told her firmly to sit down, and he put the kettle on for some tea.

'What about pills? Don't you have some?' he asked.

'Yes. But I don't need any now,' she said. 'I'm just

upset. A very old friend has died – such a shock.' She wiped her eyes. 'Perhaps two aspirins?' she said.

Ray got them for her. It gave him a chance to look at her bedroom on the way to the bathroom. Silver-backed brushes and a jewel case stood on the dressing-table for everyone to see. Careless, that was. Just asking for trouble.

She took the aspirins, and seemed calmer when she'd drunk the tea. She made Ray accept a pound when he left; he demurred just enough to create a favourable impression.

Peter Guthrie went into Floradora's to order a wreath for General Ford, and was delighted to find June in the shop, for she was his reason for making the call in person, and not by telephone.

He spent some time discussing with her what composition of blooms would be best. Then he asked her to lunch with him. Why not, thought June, after her first surprise. He was a customer; who could object?

'Thank you,' she said demurely. 'That would be nice.'

'Do you like the Hermes?' Guthrie enquired, flattering her by assuming she knew it. 'Let's meet there.'

'I don't get off till one o'clock,' she said.

'I'll have a drink waiting,' he answered.

He had: a cool, rosy Campari, with ice and a slice of lemon swimming in it.

'I hope you like this,' Guthrie said.

She did, and had made Cecil produce it as an alternative to sherry when they had had the head librarian to dinner.

'I love it,' she said.

Guthrie watched admiringly as she took off her coat, helped by a small waiter with large dark eyes and crisp black curls. She was a much better shape than Audrey.

'Have you been here before?' he asked. 'It hasn't been open long.'

'No. It's nice.' She looked around. There was a small bar at the front of the restaurant, which was decorated in mock taverna style: there was an amphora for umbrellas, vine leaves on the wall and a painting of the Parthenon among the bottles. Taped bouzouki music played softly in the background. Though not at all like a real taverna, which was an illusion impossible to achieve with the grey November day outside, it was pleasant. 'I like the music,' said June.

The waiter brought huge menus.

'Thank you, Dino,' said Guthrie, thus, as he had intended, impressing June. 'Now, what would you like?'

June studied the menu. It was written in Greek, but there were translations below each item. She said she would like to try a Greek dish.

'What first? *Dolmades?*' suggested Guthrie.

Stuffed vine leaves, read June, as Guthrie leaned across to point them out to her on the menu.

'How lovely,' she said.

They chose the rest of the meal in the same manner, with Guthrie's arm against June's as he consulted her.

'Have you been to Greece?' he asked.

'No, never.' She thought fleetingly of Barry and her thwarted trip to Corfu.

'You will, you will,' he said.

Their stuffed vine leaves arrived.

'Oh – I've had these, you can do it with cabbage leaves,' said June artlessly, turning the spiced rice over with her fork. 'But these are much better, of course,' she added hastily. 'I wonder how you get vine leaves in England?'

'Out of a tin, I expect,' said Guthrie. 'Rather an anti-climax, what?'

He actually said that: June felt an urge to giggle, but managed to resist it. She wanted to seem sophisticated. What a pity he was so old: he must be well over fifty. But he did look distinguished, and the waiters treated him with deference. It was nice. She had never been anywhere with Ted, except to a pub the second time they met, and she and Cecil seldom went out for a meal.

They drank a light white wine, well chilled.

'Felsbury's improving, having a place like this,' said Guthrie. 'It's doing well, too.'

Indeed, the restaurant was full, mostly with men.

'Business men, I suppose, all these people,' said June.

'Yes. Eating out on their expense accounts,' said Guthrie.

They both laughed, and June felt a pressure against her leg under the table. Was he really trying that corny old dodge, or was it an accident?

It was not; the pressure increased. June let her knee remain in contact and went on eating her vine leaves.

'Will you tell your husband about this?' Guthrie asked, after a short silence.

June looked at the large blue eyes in the rather red face.

'Why not?' she said. 'There's nothing wrong in going out to lunch.'

'I shan't tell my wife,' said Guthrie in meaning tones.

'Would she mind?'

'You're so pretty, my dear. She would find you a threat. What time do you have to return to the shop?'

'I don't have to go back. I only work mornings. I have to collect my children from school later on.'

'So there's no hurry? Good.'

'No, there's no hurry,' June agreed.

'You're soft,' said Charlie. 'Fancy cancelling a trip to the airport.'

'I'll get almost as much, by the time I've taken Mrs Malmesbury to the funeral, waited, and come back,' said Ted. When Mrs Malmesbury telephoned with her change of plan he had hesitated for only a moment before deciding what to do. 'Poor old soul, she doesn't want some stranger taking her to this funeral. She's known the old man most of her life.' And fancied him, Ted thought.

'You're running a business, mate, not a lonely hearts' bureau,' said Charlie.

He had come round to the mews to see if Ted had thought any more about the garage plan. He'd looked at Ted's appointment book to see how busy his prospective partner was, and had seen the scribbled changes.

'Thought any more about the garage?' Charlie asked.

Ted took the appointment book away from him and closed it.

'Yes. It's a good idea,' he said. He would have to move from Dunstable Mews soon, anyway; it was all very well to go it alone, though nice to be his own boss, answerable to no one. There were problems, if the business was to expand. He needed Charlie's workshop for his own repairs. They got on well; it made sense to join up. 'But I'd like my own place – like I've got here. It needn't be much. Just a room and a bit of plumbing.'

'We might fix something up above the garage,' said Charlie. How odd, to prefer this rough place to a comfortable room in a modern bungalow, and Doreen's cooking. Light suddenly dawned. 'It's a bird, I suppose.' He'd seen a line in the diary, drawn through tonight's times from seven o'clock until nine-fifteen. 'Seeing her tonight, are you?'

'That's right.'

'You ought to marry her, Ted. But you need a bit more than this. A proper place of your own.'

'She's married already,' said Ted.

'Oh – pity. Or maybe it's not. Suits you this way, perhaps. No responsibilities. But you'll want to settle down one day.'

'Maybe.' Ted was not to be drawn.

'Come and have another look at the place on Sunday,' said Charlie. They had been there together three times already.

'All right,' said Ted. 'That won't do any harm, I suppose. Now, do you mind pushing off? I'm expecting a visitor.'

It was ten to seven.

Charlie got up.

'Comes here, does she? She must think a lot of you.' He looked around at the bleak room.

'She doesn't come for the decor,' said Ted.

'What about her old man?'

'What he doesn't know doesn't hurt him,' said Ted.

Since she had discovered that Thursday was Cecil's late duty at the library, Lorna had taken to going there then. He was usually visible through the glass in his office.

The Thursday after she had collected the garments for the mythical jumble sale he came into the lending library while she sat reading a magazine. She was not absorbing what she read at all; she was thinking of Cecil.

He saw her, and came across.

'Ah – Miss Gibson. Good evening,' he said.

'How are the children? Was the cake a success? Did your wife like it?' The words burst from Lorna with an intensity that startled him.

'Oh yes. She guessed we'd been preparing something, of course, but she pretended it was all a great surprise,' said Cecil.

June had returned radiant from the wedding; his thoughts took a more intimate turn as they dwelt on the unexpected joys of the night that followed. She clearly thrived on meeting people; for her sake he must stifle his own preference for domesticity and take her about more. The Red Cross Ball, made possible by the plain girl sitting here, should be the first of many ventures, he decided. Meanwhile, he must take pains to be pleasant to Miss Gibson.

'What are you reading now?' he asked, and glanced at the books on the table beside her.

'I'm returning these – they were busy at the desk when I came in,' said Lorna.

Cecil picked one up.

'Guthrie, eh? Do you like his books?' He was surprised by her choice.

'I hadn't read any before, but he's one of Mr Vigors' patients. I took them from curiosity,' said Lorna. 'I didn't really enjoy them.' She hadn't been able to lose herself in the narrative. 'The hero's so very conceited.'

'You don't care for Gadsby?'

'He's heartless,' said Lorna.

'That's supposed to give him romantic appeal,' said Cecil. 'Think of Mr Rochester.'

'He had a heart,' Lorna protested. 'That was what got him into such difficulties.'

'You're right.' Cecil looked at her with more interest. 'You don't like these dominant heroes, then?'

'I don't think they'd be nice to live with,' said Lorna. 'I suppose they're all right in books, though.' She thought suddenly of Eric Sims on that hideous occasion, so confidently expecting her to submit; were all men like that? She looked at Cecil, with his mild expression, and could not believe it.

After a few more words Cecil moved off on whatever quest had brought him out of his sanctum, and Lorna sat there for quite five minutes before she was capable of getting up to hand in her books and find more.

Chapter 14

At four o'clock the following Saturday afternoon, leaving her assistant Tracy in charge of Floradora's, Joyce Watson went to have her hair done. They had spent strenuous hours earlier in the day transforming the town hall, a Victorian building in the old part of Felsbury, into a floral bower. Now it was time to prepare for the evening's revels; Joyce, like June, was going to the ball.

Tracy, left like Cinderella, had been alone in the shop for just a few minutes when a young man in jeans and an anorak entered.

'I want a pot plant for an old lady,' said Ray. 'How much is that one?' He pointed to an azalea.

Tracy told him.

'Phew! Too much! What's cheaper?'

She showed him, and he bought a bronze chrysanthemum rooted in a plastic bowl. It would last, she assured him, for ages.

'All alone here, are you?' he asked, as Tracy wrapped it up. He had been waiting outside and had seen Joyce leave.

'For a while. Mrs Watson will be back soon. She's having her hair done ready for the ball at the town hall tonight,' said Tracy, made loquacious by solitude.

'Oh yes?' This was the first Ray had heard of the ball.

'Lovely, the flowers are,' Tracy said. 'Great banks of chrysanthemums and gladioli, all yellow and white. I wish I was going.'

'What? Among all that lot? The mayor and such? Never! A disco's more your scene,' said Ray.

He paid for the plant, and as Tracy opened the till to get his change he saw that it was stuffed with notes. She noticed him looking at it, and shut it quickly. He seemed all right, but she was alone and you had to be careful.

'See you around,' he said as he left.

Mrs Floradora wouldn't leave all that money in the till overnight. Either she'd drop it at the bank, or she'd take it home. She'd be wanting to get dolled up for the ball so she would not be dawdling about. He paused in the doorway. Perhaps he should grab it now. The kid in the shop was only a bit of a thing; one clip round the ear and she'd be out cold. But the idea died as soon as born, for a man brushed past him, coming in. Ray moved on.

If the stout blonde took the cash home, he'd have plenty of time to ransack the place while she was at the ball; that was a lucky tip he'd got. On the other hand, if she meant to use the bank, there were a lot of folk about on a Saturday evening and intercepting her could be tricky. How would he know which she meant to do?

He went back to the Imp, which was in the municipal park, and put the plant on the floor. He'd gone into Floradora's on an impulse, since he already knew it was a place well worth doing, but the flowers could be used as a further means of wheedling himself into Mrs Malmesbury's good books. He'd not quite decided yet on how best to rob her, but he'd had his mother's key copied, filching it out of her handbag; she'd never missed it. He'd probably make the job look like a break-in, by doing it either at night or when the old girl was out.

He sat in the car wondering what to do about Mrs Floradora. He couldn't wait any longer. It must be tonight.

Somehow Lorna had to get through the hours till the evening. The Titmusses were to dine with the head librarian and his wife before the ball; Cecil was sure that his progress up the library ladder must be helped by this kind of event; the ways to promotion were many, and Cecil was eager to prove himself on all counts. There was no question about his professional ability; his social sense must not be found wanting either, and here June, who was seldom shy, was a priceless asset.

Lorna felt the day would never end. She was to go to The Lindens by bus, and Cecil would bring her home again. Fantasies ran through her mind about what would happen then: she would offer him tea or coffee, which he would accept, follow her upstairs and then . . . Her imagination could not cope with what came next. A blurred composite of her experience with Eric Sims and the squalid gropings of earlier years which had so disgusted her that she had speedily learned to evade them warred with scenes from modern films. The reality with Cecil would be wholly different; there would be no struggling or gasping, but some sort of instant bliss. She did not know how this could be achieved, and she told herself it would never happen, but she could not banish the idea.

How could she pass the time? She had cleaned her room, washed her hair, even cooked herself a respectable lunch for a change.

There was something she had contemplated for days; a test of herself. She would do it now.

As funerals go, Edgar's had been a good one. His contemporaries and brother officers were almost all dead, but an elderly brigadier who had been a subaltern when Edgar commanded his regiment came, and a few other old gentlemen to whom he had been a revered figure. There was a good turn-out of civilians from the village, and representatives of the British Legion and other bodies which Edgar had supported. Mrs Malmesbury had been unable to restrain her tears during 'Fight the good fight', though Hesther had remained dry-eyed throughout. Wreaths and sprays had lined the path from the church gate to the porch. All in all, the old warrior had had a splendid valedictory. Hesther's daughter, a large woman of sixty with a commanding manner, was staying to help clear things up and was then taking her mother back with her to Yorkshire, so that Mrs Malmesbury could not even aid her friend by keeping her company while she coped with lawyers and Edgar's possessions.

She had been thankful to get into the Humber, allow Ted to wrap his Black Watch rug around her, and be driven back to Cleveland Court. Ray had come the next day with the groceries, and on Friday Mrs Brett had sorted her out, as she put it, for the weekend.

Today, Saturday, Mrs Malmesbury had spoken to no one at all. She had got up later than usual, succumbing to a rare temptation to take her breakfast back to bed with her. It was a business, clambering stiffly back again, but it was cosy with the electric blanket on, and *The Times*, which arrived through her letter-box daily at eight, to read. But she'd dropped marmalade on the sheet and her coffee had dripped on to her bedjacket. In the end she had decided she must face the day, so she got up and had her bath; it was always a nerve-wracking event in case she slipped; getting out safely involved much hauling and struggling and then a sit, wrapped in a towel, on the bathroom stool while she recovered.

She was quite tired by the time she had made her bed, first sponging off the marmalade, washed up, and rinsed through some stockings and underclothes.

When her doorbell rang at three o'clock she started up from an uneasy doze. She had eaten some cheese on toast for her lunch, and sat down after that to listen to the radio, but instead she had dreamed of undefined horrors.

Who can it be, she thought crossly, reaching out for her stick and painfully levering herself to her feet. She had seen no one all day, and had now got past the point of wanting to.

A tense-looking girl stood outside in the passage. Collecting for something, probably; that meant trekking back to the sitting-room for her purse, thought Mrs Malmesbury irritably. But there was no tray of flags thrust out, nor any tin.

'Oh – Mrs Malmesbury – how are you? I came to see if you'd quite recovered,' gabbled Lorna, and as Mrs Malmesbury frowned at her, added, 'You suggested I should come again, don't you remember?'

Mrs Malmesbury still looked doubtful.

'Mr Vigors' secretary – Lorna Gibson,' Lorna prompted, desperately. She should not have come; it had been a mistake. The old thing was getting ga-ga; she prepared to flee.

But Mrs Malmesbury's life-time training came to her rescue.

'Of course I remember, how stupid of me,' she said. She would, if she really knew the girl; it would come to her in a moment or two. 'Do come in.'

She led the way, trying to adjust; of course, the girl had been here before, bringing roses, and to the hospital. She bade Lorna sit down and replied to her repeated enquiries, but finally discussions about health came to an end and they sat silent.

'Have you – have you been reading a lot?' Lorna asked, hesitantly.

'Yes. I'm reading a book about India now,' said Mrs Malmesbury. 'I was there with my husband. He was a soldier.'

Suddenly it was easy. They talked about books for half an hour. Their tastes were not similar, but Lorna had read a lot of travel books, though Mrs Malmesbury did not

126

share her enthusiasm for historical romances, and each was ready to listen to the other. Mrs Malmesbury invited the girl to stay to tea, but Lorna said she must go.

'Please don't get up. I can let myself out,' she said, as Mrs Malmesbury reached for her stick.

'I must – I get stiff if I sit too long,' said Mrs Malmesbury.

Now was the moment.

'Let me help you,' said Lorna, and she put an arm round the old lady, helping her up, then steadied her, not withdrawing her support until Mrs Malmesbury's balance was sure.

This time it was quite easy; she did not shudder at all.

Elated by this success, Lorna decided not to go straight home. She would have tea at Tansy's.

The café was busy, but she found a free table in a corner; it was laden with the debris of someone's meal, and old Mr Beauchamp came across to clear it. He did not recognize her. The elder Miss Beauchamp brought Lorna's toasted teacake and pot of tea; then three other women appeared and asked if they might share her table. Lorna almost managed a smile as they all sat down; they were absorbed in conversation and ignored her as she sat there in a sort of mental limbo. Once or twice she thought about Mrs Malmesbury, but only in relation to her own passing of the test she had set herself.

I'm not different from other people. It's just that I get no practice, she decided.

The streets were brightly lit now. Lorna looked idly at Floradora's window; beyond the display of pot plants she could see a woman with improbably blonde hair moving about at the back of the shop; a young girl was serving a customer. She sauntered on and glanced at La Boutique, where Nancy spent a lot of her pay packet; the clothes were unlike anything Lorna owned: long skirts with frills round the hem, caftans, and scooped-neck blouses. What would Mr Vigors think if Lorna were to arrive for work on Monday in a flowing skirt and a tank top? She almost laughed at the thought.

She turned away; she had filled in enough time. She started off down the road, back towards Floradora's, and crossed over the street. A young man was standing in the doorway of the betting shop, opposite the end of the zebra crossing. Lorna did not look at him particularly, but he moved as she passed, pushed by someone coming out of the betting shop behind him, and Lorna swerved to avoid a collision.

She was not on her bicycle this time, but it was the second occasion when that had happened; this was the young man she had seen before and described to Detective Chief Inspector Purdy: the one with the very pale eyes.

'How's that girl of yours? The prunes and prisms one who won't touch anyone,' said Susan Vigors. She sat in front of her dressing-table, her thick hair falling around her naked shoulders, her skin creamy above the black lace of her expensive new evening bra.

Bryan came up behind her, wrapped his arm round her neck, and laid his bearded face against her cheek, then looked at their reflections in the mirror.

'Better. Even speaks, sometimes, before she's spoken to. And has nearly smiled. Why do you ask?'

'I just wondered. I felt sorry for her, all of a sudden,' said Susan.

'Why? And why now?' Bryan slid his hands under Susan's bra. 'I wish you wouldn't wear these fortifications,' he grumbled.

'I must, darling. You don't want me unconfined,

pressed against the mayor, surely?' said Susan. She brushed his beard with her hairbrush, caressingly.

Bryan nuzzled her neck instead of answering.

'Bryan, stop. Not again. There isn't time,' said Susan.

'There's always time,' said Bryan.

Their bed was still rumpled, for they had left it only a short while before. The children were spending the night with their grandparents and there was no one else to be thought of, just themselves.

Susan did not protest for long. Sliding her arms round his broad shoulders she murmured. 'This is why I'm sorry for poor Miss Prisms. She doesn't know about this.'

'Damn Miss Prisms,' said Bryan. 'Who cares about her?'

Chapter 15

'I'll let her in, I'll let her in,' cried Barty.

The children were looking forward to the novelty of having Lorna in charge of them, and since the episode of his toy car, Barty had regarded her as his special property.

'She doesn't talk down to them,' Cecil explained to June, who had been told of Lorna's presence during the icing of her birthday cake.

In fact Lorna had had so little to do with children that she knew no way of addressing them except as equals. Now, as she rang the bell and waited outside the door of The Lindens' she heard scuffling from within, and realized with some relief that the children were not yet in bed. She was in a high state of excitement, but she was apprehensive about meeting June.

The door opened, and there stood Barty in his dressing-gown, his hair brushed and his face shining with cleanliness.

'Hullo, Barty,' said Lorna, and as the little boy lifted his face to her, she bent down and kissed him. It seemed the natural thing to do.

'Ah, Miss Gibson. There you are, then,' said Cecil, rather heartily.

'Please call me Lorna,' she begged.

'Lorna, then.'

Cecil felt self-conscious in his dinner jacket, but Lorna thought he looked elegant, if remote; he smelt faintly of after-shave, although in fact Lorna did not realize that that was what it was.

'The children begged to stay up till you came,' he said.

'I hope I'm not late?' She suddenly panicked. She could not have made a mistake in the time; in fact she had spent five minutes pacing up and down the road outside until the exact appointed hour arrived.

'No, no. Punctual to the minute.'

Janet had been hovering in the background during this exchange; she did not rush eagerly at Lorna, as her brother had done but was assessing her coolly.

'Your supper's ready,' she said now. 'Chicken and cherry flan, and sherry.'

'Oh, you shouldn't have bothered,' Lorna said.

'There's a long night ahead. You'll need something,' said Cecil.

There was a flurry from above, and June came down the stairs. She wore an apricot-coloured dress with a gold pattern woven into the fabric, which glowed and rustled as she moved. Her hair was coiled in a knot on top of her head, from which it fell in a shining swathe on her neck. Above the rounded neckline of her dress her flesh was soft and white. All four watchers caught their breath at the sight of her.

June was smiling as she made her entrance: then she saw Lorna, and froze.

'Oh,' she said, and stopped on the stairs 'So you're Miss Gibson.'

'You've met?' said Cecil.

Lorna felt a surge of power at what she could do, and, suddenly decisive after weeks of doubt, knew at once how to answer.

'Yes,' she said. 'It was at Italian classes. I haven't kept them up. I only went twice.' It was a lie; she had attended three lessons but June gave up after two.

June began floating down the stairs again.

'I know,' she said, all smiles once more. 'What a pity.' She came on, and arrived in the hall.

'What a beautiful dress,' said Lorna, quite sincerely.

She's nice, she thought later, when the children were in bed. She had never expected to like June, but it was impossible not to, in a way. June had fussed about, making sure that Lorna knew how to switch on the television; showed her where the tea was kept, and the instant coffee; told her to make herself at home and have as much sherry as she liked; and thanked her profusely for coming. Lorna did not realize that some of this effusiveness might be due to relief after the shock of recognition and Lorna's subsequent reassurance.

June and Cecil had left almost at once, and Lorna had played with the children, then read to them, and finally tucked them into bed, receiving another kiss from Barty and a reserved but friendly goodnight from Janet. After that she had sat by the gas fire, in the very chair that Cecil used when making his models, breathing in the atmosphere of his home. For a long time she forgot all about June.

She had eaten the chicken and cherry flan eventually, and drunk the sherry.

After that she'd gone upstairs and looked at the children. Both were fast asleep, Barty with the giraffe's threadbare cheek close to his own.

Then, greatly daring, she went into the main bedroom.

There was their bed, a very ordinary double divan. It was turned down, with June's nightdress, a mauve wisp, on one pillow, and Cecil's green cotton pyjamas on the other. Lorna looked round at the white-painted fitments, the small upholstered chair, the heavy mahogany chest of drawers on which a man's hairbrush and comb and three ballpoint pens in different colours were aligned in a row.

The implications of these details were too much for her, and she left the room quickly; it was more comfortable to reflect on the scenes of domesticity she had witnessed.

At eleven o'clock she remembered the young man with the pale blue eyes whom she had seen outside the betting shop. There had been no time, afterwards, to ring Chief Inspector Purdy, for the rest of her day was carefully mapped out and nothing must jeopardize those arrangements.

Ray reasoned it out again. The blonde would not leave the money in Floradora's over the weekend, and she could not lock it up elsewhere in the building, for the floors above the shop were filled by the offices of Messrs Hope and Synge, solicitors. She would be taking it either home or to the bank night safe; all he had to do was follow her, and look for a moment when he might grab it; she would not be expecting an assault; it should be easy.

He waited, lurking in the shadows near the betting office, and saw the girl who had served him in the florist's come out and walk away on her platform soles. Ten minutes later the older woman appeared; she carried a large holdall.

Ray followed behind her as she set off up the road.

They went through the Buttermarket, up Manor Road, and into Chester Street; this was not the route to the bus-stop; she must be going to the Midland Bank, which was round the next corner; it was now or never that he must intercept her.

He could not stop in the street to put on his stocking mask. He pulled his cap down over his eyes, and took from his pocket the weapon that he had prepared: a stone wrapped in a sock. Joyce never knew what hit her. She sank to the ground without a sound; Ray seized her holdall and was gone, running down a side street, not slowing up until he reached a deserted alley-way a quarter of a mile away. Then, panting hard, he opened the holdall.

It was there: a worn leather bag just like the others. He thrust it inside his jacket front where it made a large bulge. There was a handbag in the holdall too, and he looked in that. Among a lot of clutter there was a fat purse; it held at least thirty pounds, and he took that too. Then he tossed holdall and handbag over a nearby wall and walked off, not too fast, to where he had left his car.

Superintendent Whitchurch had spent Saturday afternoon in the garden, sweeping up the last of the leaves which had lain about soggily for weeks. A bonfire smoked at the end of his quarter-acre plot, the smell of it tangy in the cold wintry air. Inside the house Mrs Whitchurch was ironing her evening dress, the same brown wild silk one, trimmed with velvet, which had been her best for several years. The Whitchurches were going to the ball.

Mrs Whitchurch was looking forward to it; for once it seemed as if they would get there on time. Usually Dan was called out just as they were getting ready; she sometimes basely suspected him of fixing it up in advance, since he hated such formal occasions. Anyway, he had spent a peaceful afternoon undisturbed among the apple trees.

She looked through the kitchen window. It was dark outside; he must be scarcely able to see what he was doing out there.

She finished ironing the dress, took it upstairs and hung it outside her wardrobe; she still took the same size as twenty years ago, a matter for modest complacence. Next year she really must have something new; she must talk to Dan about it.

He came in at last, the smell of smoke clinging to him, his grey hair tousled and with colour in his usually pale face. The afternoon had done him good.

'Well, dear? All set for the bunfight?' he asked.

'We should be getting ready, Dan. The Hodges have asked us for seven.'

The Whitchurches were to dine with Dr and Mrs Hodge; he was the police surgeon.

'I'll go up. I need a bath,' said Dan.

He was still in it, washing the traces of twigs and smoke out of his hair, when they telephoned from the police station.

The mayor received the guests at the top of the stairs leading into the huge upstairs room at the town hall, with his mayoress, plump in purple, beside him.

June felt rather shy. It was the first time she and Cecil had been to so grand a function. But one look at the assembled company restored her confidence. Nearly all the women were almost twice her age, and most were three sizes fatter; she had never looked better than now, and on that score alone she need fear nobody.

It had been a nasty moment when she recognized Lorna, and surprising to learn that she had given up the classes, for she had seemed so keen. But she seemed to be all that Cecil had said, a perfect baby-sitter.

Cecil was feeling timid; both were glad to be under the wing of the head librarian and his wife, but Cecil had seen at a glance that there was no woman in the room to equal June. She was almost too beautiful, he thought, in a moment of uneasiness as the head librarian swept her off to dance.

Circling round in Mr Gregson's respectful grasp, June looked over his barathea shoulder watching for Peter Guthrie, whom she knew was coming. It had been disclosed during the drive they had taken together after their lunch. He had stopped the car in a lonely lane, laid a hand on her thigh and his lips on hers, and suggested that they should visit a motel not far away.

June, filled with a sense of power, had removed his hand, drawn back from his searching mouth, and asked: 'Why?'

'Because you're a woman and I'm a man,' said Guthrie, quoting his hero Gadsby.

June almost giggled.

'No,' she said.

'Because of your husband?' he asked, again echoing Gadsby.

'What makes you think I'd agree?' asked June, prevaricating.

'It would be good for us both,' said Guthrie.

It sounded so clinical. And he was so old. It was not a temptation at all. Ted had only to touch her to make her feel as though she must dissolve; she felt nothing like that now, just a desire to laugh. Did he really think her a pushover? She had been for Ted, of course; but that was different.

However, she wouldn't slap him down utterly; more lunches like today's would be nice, and she could learn a lot from him without letting herself be seduced. She could let him hope on for a while, and escape when he had worn out his usefulness; through him, she might meet other people.

'But I hardly know you,' she said.

'We'll change all that,' said Guthrie.

Silly old fool, thought June.

He had been pleased that she and Cecil would be at the ball. Cecil already knew that they had met at the wedding, so there was no need to hide that. But tonight, with the Gregsons, they had dined at the Hermes, and she had a moment's anxiety in case the waiter recognized her and made some comment. Not that it mattered, really, but Cecil might think it strange that she should go out to lunch with Guthrie and not tell him about it.

The dance ended, and Mr Gregson took her to join his wife and Cecil. A moment later Guthrie came over to their table. He knew the Gregsons, and greeted everyone, but it was at June that he gazed.

'Will you join us?' asked Mr Gregson.

Guthrie did, forgetting all about his wife. He talked

about the ball, the state of the town and its redevelopment, and the crime wave. He scarcely drew breath, his powerful voice booming out so that no one else could speak, and all the time his eyes were on June.

Does he really think he'll win? June marvelled. I can do better than that. If I want to.

Ted saw June arrive at the ball. He was busy that night driving people to the town hall, and as he arrived on his second trip the familiar Morris stopped ahead of him. Cecil sprang out from the driver's seat and rushed round to the passenger's side. An unknown woman got out, while June and a man emerged from the back. June wore a cloak, so he did not see the full splendour of her dress, but her hair, arranged as it was, made her look very elegant. Turning to talk to the man at her side she faced Ted, but did not see him. Or if she did, she gave no sign.

When he had finished delivering people to the ball he went straight to the telephone and rang up Charlie.

'I'll come in with you, on that garage,' he said. 'The sooner the better.'

Superintendent Whitchurch reached the ball in the end, although without any dinner. When he arrived, his wife and their friends Dr and Mrs Hodge were talking to Bryan and Susan Vigors.

'What kept you?' asked Vigors.

'Woman been hit on the head,' said Whitchurch. 'Found lying on the pavement in Chester Street.'

'How dreadful,' exclaimed Mrs Hodge. 'Who is she?'

'We don't know yet. Her bag had gone. We'll find out more when she's missed from home. Purdy's dealing with it.'

'You haven't seen her?'

'She's in the operating theatre.'

'Bad, eh?' This from the doctor.

'Very. Fractured skull – she's in a critical state.'

'Put a damper on your evening, hasn't it?' said Vigors.

'Deprived me of my dinner, anyway,' said Whitchurch. 'I'm famished. Any food going here?'

Vigors bore him off to the buffet and nibbled a sandwich while the policeman tucked into salmon mayonnaise.

'Woman going to die, Dan?'

'Can't tell yet. Hope not.'

'You'll be on to me, I suppose, if you can't find out who she is. I wouldn't like to think one of my patients had got mugged in Felsbury – or anywhere else, come to that.'

'Plenty of other dentists in the town, Bryan,' said Whitchurch. 'She may not be one of yours. Anyway, there's sure to be a missing call for her soon. Smartly dressed, middle-aged woman.'

'Very nasty,' said Vigors. 'Makes you think it might have been your own wife. You're sure it was only robbery?'

'No signs of anything else.'

'Hm.' Vigors looked gloomy.

'It wasn't very far from the bank where that publican was attacked in October,' said Whitchurch. 'Then the old fellow from the tea shop was robbed later. There might be a connection.'

'You'd rather be out there helping than at this affair, wouldn't you?' Vigors asked.

'You're right,' said Whitchurch. 'But Purdy can get on with it. Doesn't do to breathe down his neck all the while. He knows where to find me.'

'I'd rather have my job than yours,' said the dentist.

When Whitchurch had finished eating they returned to the ballroom, passing the table where Cecil and Audrey Guthrie were sitting. Cecil had rescued Audrey when it was clear that her husband had abandoned her. She was a constant visitor to the library for she did a lot of her husband's research. Like Guthrie she was Vigors' patient, and the dentist stopped to greet her. Cecil recognized the big bearded man; he had often seen him getting out of his Volvo outside the surgery, though they had never met.

'Your Miss Gibson is baby-sitting for us tonight,' he said.

'Good heavens! Is she?' Vigors was amazed. He and Susan had never thought of asking the surgery staff to undertake that duty.

'A nice girl,' said Cecil.

Vigors was so surprised by this that he told Susan about it, and brought her over to join Cecil and Audrey. Guthrie himself and June, who had been together most of the evening, had returned to the table and June agreed that Lorna seemed likely to be an excellent baby-sitter.

'The children like her,' she said.

'I scarcely know her,' said Susan. 'Bryan's been holding out on me.'

She smiled at June in a friendly fashion. She was one of those rare, warm-hearted creatures, sublimely confident, secure and fulfilled in her own marriage, who was willing to believe the best about everyone else and make friendly overtures in most directions.

Later, in the cloakroom, she said to June, 'Old hot hands never gives up, does he?'

'Who?'

'Peter Guthrie. Mr Grope himself,' said Susan.

June felt her face stiffen. Susan was putting on lipstick, her mouth stretched wide, peering at herself in the spotted town hall mirror; the cloakroom facilities in that civic building were not very splendid.

'Thinks he's irresistible,' Susan went on, without waiting for June's reply. 'We had them to dinner one night. I think he expected, as we're younger, that it was

139

going to be a swapping party or something. He must have been most disappointed. She's nice, though.'

'Oh – yes, she is,' said June, floundering.

'Silly old fool,' said Susan comfortably. 'One can't tell him to get lost, though, since he's a patient, I suppose.'

'Does he – does – er –?' June did not know quite how to phrase her question.

'Does anyone fall for his line? I doubt it,' said Susan. 'Not a second time, anyway. In, out, and then, "God, that was wonderful" and straight to sleep'd be his style, I bet, but I'm not planning to find out.'

June was slightly shocked but enthralled by this speech. Such conversations were not typical of the exchanges she had with other young women.

Susan was still talking.

'Your husband is so kind,' she said. 'Do you know, he saw poor Mrs Guthrie left all alone and rescued her? Bryan would think of it, but he'd be too busy chatting to do it himself. We're having a party soon. You must come to it.'

'Thank you,' said June. 'We'd love to.'

'Get Lorna to baby-sit,' giggled Susan.

'Yes.'

Cecil was kind; that was true.

Chapter 16

Lorna drowsed by the gas fire. The sherry had made her sleepy. She had explored the whole of the house: the spare-bedroom, rather bare; and the sitting-room, clearly seldom used, which had dove-grey walls, brass-mounted wall lights, and two Canaletto prints.

She tried pretending that she lived here; any minute now Cecil would return, alone. She would make tea and they would discuss the day's events. It was not an impossible dream: June might leave him, and then he would need someone to look after both him and the children.

What would he do if he knew the truth? June did not deserve all this – the children, the house, her security; most of all, Cecil. Yet if she left, they would be desolate.

It was half-past one when they returned from the ball. Cecil had instructed her to put up the chain and said he would give two short rings when they got back, but she heard the car before the bell.

June came in first, laughing and flushed, a tendril of hair that had escaped from the knot on top of her head curling against her cheek. Cecil followed, and automatically bolted the door. They brought in a hint of crisp, wintry night.

'I'm afraid we're terribly late, Lorna. You must be exhausted,' said June.

'Oh no!' said Lorna. 'I've been perfectly happy.' It was true. 'And the children have been so good – not a sound, after they went to bed.'

'You'll want to get back.'

She didn't, but she must. Cecil looked tired, and every moment that prolonged her pleasure increased his fatigue. Besides, he must want to be with June: yes, looking at her and then at him, he must.

'I'll get my coat,' she said.

'Unzip me, Cecil, before you go,' said June, and smiling to herself she turned her back to Cecil, who slid the zip carefully down. For a moment his hand hovered above her bare back, but all he said was, 'There, dear,' and added, 'Ready, then?' to Lorna.

She noticed that he did not remind June to set the chain on the door after they had gone. He would not be long, and June would not want to come down again to let him in. She'd be busy putting on that wisp of a nightie.

There was very little traffic about, but a police car with its light flashing went past as they drove towards the town centre.

'Some woman got coshed in Chester Street tonight,' said Cecil. 'You should be careful, Lorna, riding your bicycle.'

'I'm safer on that than walking,' she said, but she glowed. Fancy him even bothering to caution her.

At her door, he pressed a pound into her hand.

'I don't want it, really,' she said. 'It was a pleasure.'

'If you don't take it, we'll feel we can't ask you again,' said Cecil.

'Well, all right then. Thank you,' she said.

'Goodbye,' said Cecil, and drove off before she had unlocked her door.

He couldn't wait to get back to June.

A hospital porter recognized Joyce when she was wheeled back from the theatre after an emergency operation.

'You're sure?' asked the staff nurse in charge.

'Certain,' answered the man. 'She's come here with flowers before now, though usually it's a girl that drives the van.'

The policewoman who had been left at the hospital got in touch with the station, and Purdy was soon round there. He brought one of the Miss Beauchamps with him as being the first person he could think of who might confirm the identification, for the shops were so close that the ladies must be acquainted. Miss Olga agreed that she knew Mrs Watson quite well, and knew too that she had planned to go to the ball.

'Not alone, surely?' asked Purdy. 'Where's her husband?'

'She's divorced,' said Miss Beauchamp. 'But she has an – er – a friend.'

'Hm. Wonder why he didn't ask questions when she didn't turn up?'

'It does seem strange.' Privately Miss Beauchamp thought the irregularity of the relationship was the reason. But it was none of her business. And she was shaken at the sight of poor Joyce, her head wrapped in bandages, her face waxen; she had always seemed a tough character and now she was utterly reduced.

Purdy took her back home and went round to the town hall to find Superintendent Whitchurch, who was only too delighted to leave the ball and supervise the hunt for Joyce's assailant.

Ray drove right out into the country before he broke open the bank bag. It was as tough as the others had been, made of strong old leather, and he forced the lock, as he had before. There was over three hundred pounds in cash in it, and a lot of cheques; they were no good to him, and he cursed, but there was nothing wrong with the money. He put the cheques back in the bag, tossed it over a nearby hedge and drove back to town. There, hungry after his exertions, he went to a Wimpey bar and had beefburgers and chips. After that he went off to the cinema; he liked a film after a job, it gave him a chance to relax.

He gave only a cursory thought to his victim; she would have recovered quickly, just as the others had done, and with no more idea than they had what he looked like.

Lorna slept very little in what was left of the night, and when she did, feverish dreams pursued her. She saw Janet and Barty fleeing down some sort of dark tunnel, screaming; there was Ted Jessop in a dinner jacket; and Cecil in prison overalls. She woke with a headache.

Sunday dawned clear and cold. She could not go round to spy on The Lindens so soon after being part of the household; anyway, during daylight, there was little to see except in summer when the family went into the garden. Dusk was the best time, when the lights went on, before the curtains were drawn.

She would go out for the day on her bicycle. The weather was fine. In summer she rode miles at weekends; there was no need to talk to a soul. She always took sandwiches; then she need not go into a pub.

At half-past eleven, with her head now clear but her face chilled from pedalling along in the cold air, she reached Diddington.

It was a small village, with a cluster of cottages near a pond, a church with a square tower, two or three larger houses and some outlying farms, and a crop of modern close-packed uniform brick boxes. There was a pub opposite the pond, and a few cars were parked near the church.

Lorna got off her bicycle and left it among them, leaning against the churchyard wall, then walked through the gate and up the path. The sound of singing reached her. She had forgotten that a service might be in progress; she liked church buildings, but knew little of the ritual that went on within. It struck her that she and Cecil shared a fondness for ecclesiastical architecture; she must cultivate it in herself. The library would be sure to have plenty of books on the subject, and Cecil might even advise her.

The singing stopped, and was succeeded by a low rumble of voices. Lorna turned away from the path and began to wander among the tombstones. A patch of colour caught her eye; it was a recent grave, covered with flowers; the cold had preserved them and most of them still looked fresh. Fancy so many people sending you flowers, she thought. The dead person must have had many friends. 'To dear Edgar, in loving memory, Dorothy,' she read on one.

'Aren't they lovely?' said someone behind her.

Lorna had thought herself alone; she was startled at the voice.

'I'm sorry, I made you jump,' said the speaker, who was a faded-looking woman in a brown tweed coat, wearing an angora woollen hat. She was a patient of Mr Vigors.

'Poor old General Ford. He was over ninety,' said the woman, while Lorna strove to remember her name. She smiled at the girl, whom she recognized and thought must be from the village. 'I've slipped out of church early,' she went on. 'We've people coming to lunch.' She looked at Lorna more closely. 'I do know you, don't I?' she asked uncertainly.

'Yes. I'm Mr Vigors' receptionist.'

'Ah, that's it, of course. I'm Audrey Guthrie.'

Of course! Her teeth were not strong; she had several gold crowns and Guthrie had delayed paying for the last one.

'I came over on my bicycle,' Lorna said.

'How energetic. Aren't you tired?'

'No, not at all.'

'Come back with me and have a drink. In fact, stay to lunch,' said Audrey.

'Oh, I couldn't!' Lorna sought for an excuse. 'My clothes – I'm not dressed for –'

'You look very nice,' Audrey cut in. 'And I shall change into trousers. Do come. You'll liven us up – a new face. Just what we need.'

'But your friends –'

'The more the merrier,' said Audrey, now determined that the girl should accept.

Lorna gave in.

'Well, thank you,' she said.

'Willoughby Cottage,' said Audrey. 'Just past The Rose and Crown, on the other side of the road. I'll go ahead, as I've got the car. Oh, what's your name?'

Lorna told her.

Driving off, Audrey wondered what on earth had made her ask the girl. At first she'd thought her some mourner, staring rapt at the flowers on Edgar's grave; she'd looked so forlorn. But one couldn't really be sad about Edgar, poor old boy; he'd had a good run, and a very long one, which had ended peacefully. Perhaps it was something about the solitary aspect of the girl which had struck an answering chord in Audrey, who went to church not from conviction or duty, but to escape, for Peter seldom followed her there.

The evening before, at the Red Cross ball, he had made a fool of himself peering down the fronts of Susan Vigors' and the Titmuss girl's dresses: appropriately named, the latter, thought Audrey with rare savagery as she put away the car. Both young women must think him a lecherous old idiot.

He had spent the morning reading the paper and then an advance copy of his next book, just arrived from the publisher. When she came into the house he instantly challenged her.

'You missed a double print on page thirty-six,' he said. 'Look, the word *off* is written twice.'

'You missed it too,' said Audrey.

She typed his manuscripts, read his proofs after he had been through them, did a lot of his research and kept up a file of the characters recurring in each series. He had never heard her answer back like this before, and he looked at her in astonishment.

'That's a fine spirit to come back from church in, I must say,' was his comment.

Audrey took no notice. She went upstairs, changed from her jersey dress into a pair of slacks, and pulled on a long waistcoat over a sweater. Then the doorbell rang.

'It's my guest,' she said, rushing past Peter with unusual speed to open the door.

For once he was speechless as he saw his wife admitting to the house a girl he thought he did not know, and whom he certainly had not said might be invited.

Audrey bore Lorna away to wash, telling her to come downstairs when she was ready. There wasn't much that she could do to improve her appearance, but she took the band off her hair and shook it loose on her shoulders. Guthrie was not to be seen when she went downstairs; in fact he was sulking in his study. Audrey gave her a glass of sherry and listened with a smile to her shy but enthusiastic praise of the house, which was old, with leaded lights and low, beamed ceilings.

'Have you lived here long?' asked Lorna.

'Ten years. Since Peter started to do well with his books.'

Audrey could never understand why he was so successful. His books sold in thousands all over Europe and in America. Sometimes she thought if she had to type another line about Gadsby leering at the adjutant's bride or some other naive female she would go mad. His forays in the field were not much more enlivening than his amorous skirmishes; he was always reckless but triumphant under fire, much given to oaths and to sweating. The new tank series would be just the same; only the time and the setting would alter.

When the other visitors arrived, Guthrie emerged from the study, pretending he had spent the morning creating.

'Don't know how you do it,' said his friend, who was bluff and hearty, and rather like Guthrie. The wife had iron-grey hair swept severely back; she wore green leather trousers, a shaggy long cardigan and a great many bangles and bracelets which clattered on her arm.

Guthrie carved the roast pork. The vegetables were placed on the table and everyone helped themselves. Lorna had not eaten such a meal for years. She scarcely spoke; there was no need, for the two men were talking about money, and the women were discussing holidays. Audrey, anxious to include Lorna in the conversation, saw that she was savouring every morsel of food; she noticed the thin hands, the gaunt bones of the girl's face. The child's half-starved, she thought, aghast.

The woman cleared away, and Audrey showed Lorna how to load the dishwasher.

'And what do you do?' the shaggy cardigan lady asked Lorna. She draped herself decoratively in front of the boiler and regarded the girl without much interest.

'Secretarial work,' said Lorna, but the woman barely waited for her reply. She began to tell Audrey about her daughter who was living in Turkey with some sort of drop-out.

'I didn't want to tell you in front of the men, Audrey,' she said. 'Hugh practically bursts a blood vessel if you mention her name.'

Lorna busied herself wiping the table and polishing

glasses while the other women discussed their children. The three young Guthries were away, one at university, one working in Toronto, and the third, who was still at school, was visiting a friend.

'They use home like a hotel. I know,' said shaggy-cardigan.

'Mine are happier away,' said Audrey. 'Peter's so strict. I sometimes think he lives in the time of Gadsby.'

'They weren't so strict then, my dear. That came later,' said the other woman.

These women were both unhappy. The visitor was rich; the car outside, even to Lorna's ignorant eye, oozed money from every chrome or cellulose inch. The Guthries might not be in the same income bracket, but they were not short of money; you had only to look at their kitchen. Yet with all that they had, they were no better off than she was.

She had plenty to think of as she rode home. On consecutive days she had been briefly involved with two very different households. Today she had carried away no sense of family unity or happiness, but at The Lindens there was love; Cecil loved June, and both parents loved their children.

Something so rare should not be jeopardized.

Chapter 17

The police were able to get into Joyce Watson's bungalow without breaking in as her neighbour had a key. A letter, unstamped, lay on the mat.

Whitchurch opened it, then showed it to Purdy.

'Some of us are pretty fair bastards,' he said.

The letter was signed 'Jack', and said in brief terms that the writer thought, all in all, it would be better if he did not see Joyce any more. He was moving his job and would be living up north; sorry, and thanks.

'Stood her up for the dance as well,' said Purdy. 'What a sod. Maybe he was the one who did her.'

'Well – he'd have known her habits – what she did with her weekend takings. But I fancy it's connected with those two other robberies. We must find this Jack, though. Get round next door and see what's known about him, Bob. He must have been a frequent caller – maybe you can find out what sort of car he has – even his surname.'

'It could be Jack who did the other two jobs,' said Purdy.

'He's a young chap, according to your Miss Gibson.'

'Doesn't rule him out. Mrs Watson may fancy them young.'

'She'll be lucky if she fancies anyone after this lot,' grunted Whitchurch. 'And if he had anything to do with this business, he'd hardly have left a lead like this sitting here, waiting.'

Purdy had to agree. He went round to the neighbour's house and learned quite a lot about Jack. He was fifty and flashy, she said, turning down the corners of her mouth disapprovingly. She wasn't at all surprised to hear he'd gone off; many a time she'd warned poor Joyce that he was no good, but she'd expected that he would eventually get a divorce and marry her. The neighbour thought he was just out for what he could get, unlikely to return to the wife he allegedly had, and reluctant to shoulder any other responsibility.

'Joyce had a nice place here. He could hang up his hat whenever he liked. He's area manager for some hardware firm. Hughes, his surname is.'

Purdy went back to Joyce's bungalow and reported all this. Whitchurch, meanwhile, had found nothing of interest in the papers in Joyce's desk.

'There are several assistants in the flower shop,' Purdy said. 'According to the neighbour, Mrs Watson thought a lot of one of them – a June Titmuss. Part-time but trained and efficient. It's not known where she lived – somewhere in town.'

'Ah. Well, I suppose someone had better see her. She'll know what Mrs Watson did with the money. Try the telephone directory, Bob. There can't be too many people with that name.'

There were three Titmusses in Felsbury, and the third one that Purdy rang was Cecil. Over the telephone he merely established that Mrs Titmuss of that address did work at Floradora's.

'Right. I'll be over directly,' said Purdy briskly.

It was only nine o'clock. Janet and Barty had woken at their usual hour, but their parents felt far from alert after their late night. June had been awake when Cecil got back from taking Lorna home; she had left the bedside light on, and her eyes glittered as she watched him undress. Neither spoke. He put his money in neat piles as usual, and hung up his hired dinner jacket. When he got into bed he leaned across and kissed her cheek.

'You looked lovely tonight. Thank you,' he said, and rolled away from her, turning his back on temptation. She must be as tired as he was.

He was soon asleep, but June lay wakeful for a long time. She woke heavy-headed next morning, and was still in her dressing-gown when the police telephoned.

'Go up and put some clothes on, dear,' said Cecil. 'You can't talk to the police like that.'

Her hair was dishevelled, and her bare toes stuck out of her mules. Cecil was worried; there was trouble of some sort, and it was connected with June; the police had asked for her, not him. Perhaps she had committed a driving offence.

June, too, was uneasy. She could not think why the police wanted to see her, and because of Ted her conscience was not clear. It was better to be dressed, and wearing lipstick, for any sort of confrontation.

As the police car stopped outside she came down the stairs in black slacks and a tight-fitting black sweater.

'Proper knock-out, she is, that Mrs Titmuss,' was Purdy's driver's comment, back at the station.

The Chief Inspector's interview did not take long. He broke the news of the attack on Joyce and asked what she usually did with the money. June said that she varied it, sometimes taking it home, but sometimes using the night safe. She would probably have used the safe the night before as she was going to the ball. Only then did June realize that she had not seen Joyce at the town hall; she had been so busy enjoying herself that she had not looked for her.

'Tracy Brown might know what she did yesterday. She works full-time in the shop,' said June.

She knew where Tracy lived, and Purdy wrote the address down.

'Can we do anything? Help at all?' asked Cecil.

'No, I'm afraid not. It's up to the doctors,' said Purdy.

Cecil had banished the children out of earshot, but they returned when the policeman left wanting to know why he had come.

'Mrs Watson at the shop has been hurt in an accident,' said June.

'June!' Cecil said, in a warning tone.

'Oh Cecil, they'll have to know. People do get hurt and kids must realize it,' said June.

'Was she run over?' asked Barty.

'No. A bad man hit her on the head,' said June. 'Now you know why you mustn't talk to strangers.'

Perhaps he should leave at once, Ray thought: put miles between himself and Felsbury. He'd got a lot of money now, enough to last for quite a while. But they'd be looking for whoever attacked that woman. If he disappeared without warning it might look suspicious. Best wait a few days till the hue and cry had died down, as it had after the other two jobs. He could give his notice in at Crawley's and tell his parents he was off: then no one would wonder, when he did go. Besides, there was still Mrs Malmesbury.

There were plenty of pickings in that flat of hers; he'd seen her wearing a great big ring, diamonds, most likely; and she must have more stuff hidden away. He'd go round at night; she wouldn't wear her jewels in bed.

Sundays were a drag. If he fancied a bit of skirt he'd got to go looking for it, since he'd finished with Brenda. She'd got a new fellow now, he'd heard from his mother, who'd told him about it reproachfully.

'You did ought to have made it up with her. A nice girl, Brenda is,' said Mrs Brett.

'Plenty more about,' said Ray, and went off to buy the *News of the World*, which he read until dinner time, while a smell of roasting meat filled the flat. He had to admit that his mum was a dab hand at providing a tasty meal. Best eat free at home, and then clear off. He'd go to Bristol for the day, where there'd be some talent if he looked for it. And he'd leave the car there for a bit, just in case some nosey bloke had seen it near the spot where Joyce Watson was found.

Chapter 18

'Rinse, please,' said Vigors.

The patient spat into the bowl at his side. Before resuming what he was doing, Vigors cast an irritated glance above the uneasy head of the man in the chair to where Lorna sat at the desk in the corner of the surgery, staring at the wall in front of her in an apparent fit of abstraction. He had never found her lacking in concentration before. Nancy had gone out on an urgent errand, and Lorna was meanwhile acting as nurse. Lately, she had seemed less detached and had been better with the patients; Vigors had felt she was overcoming whatever block it was that inhibited her, but today she was not even efficient; she mixed the wrong filling, and she dropped a kidney bowl.

The patient left, and before the next one came in, Vigors asked her if she felt ill.

'No, I'm quite well,' said Lorna.

'Well, take a grip on yourself, then, Lorna. You're miles away,' said Vigors.

'I'm sorry,' said Lorna.

She wished Nancy would return so that she could escape to the office and think. It was from Nancy that she had learned of the attack on Joyce Watson, who still lay critically ill in the hospital. Round and round in Lorna's brain went the thought that she had seen Mr Beauchamp's attacker on Saturday evening but had done nothing about it. If she had told the police, Joyce might have escaped. For it must have been the same man who had attacked her. And she'd seen him again yesterday: at least she'd thought so afterwards: on the way back from Diddington.

If Joyce Watson died, it would be her fault.

She had still done nothing by lunch time, when Nancy stayed in the office munching a Bounty bar and eating strawberry yoghurt, a diet that made Lorna's stomach turn over.

'It just shows that no one's safe,' said Nancy. 'You should be careful, Lorna, in that place of yours all on your own. It'd give me the creeps, living like that. No one else in the building, and all that paint below. What if it caught fire?'

It was something that Lorna had never considered.

'They're careful, I suppose,' she said. Maybe that was why her rent was low, compared with what other people paid. 'And no one's going to attack me. Why should they want to?'

Nancy could think of a reason, but it might be wiser to keep quiet. Lorna was so strange; fancy not sharing with someone – it would be so much cheaper as well as more fun.

'Wonder if she'll be all right,' she said aloud. 'It's awful to think of her lying there, all bashed up. I'd often seen her in the shop. Hadn't you?'

'The blonde woman?'

'That's right. Wonder if they'll find out who did it.'

'I hope so,' Lorna said.

She called at the police station after work and asked for Chief Inspector Purdy. He was out.

'When will he be back?'

'I couldn't say. What would be the trouble, miss?' asked the sergeant at the desk.

It was all too complicated to explain to a stranger.

'How – how is Mrs Watson?' she asked. 'Do you know? The woman who was attacked on Saturday.'

156

'Still unconscious,' said the sergeant. 'Why? Is she a friend of yours?'

'No – not really. I just wondered,' said Lorna. 'It doesn't matter.'

She was turning away when a door opened at the back of the area where the sergeant was working, and an older man appeared.

'Chief Inspector Purdy not back yet?' he asked the sergeant.

'No, sir. This young lady was just asking for him,' said the sergeant. 'She was enquiring about Mrs Watson.'

Superintendent Whitchurch looked sharply at Lorna. They had not met, but she had been described to him and he had seen her photograph in the *Felsbury Gazette*.

'Miss Gibson, isn't it?'

'Yes – I –'

'Come along in and tell me what's on your mind,' said the superintendent.

Ray had left the car in a multi-storey park in Bristol and come back by train on Sunday evening, after what seemed to him a wasted day.

Once the blonde was out of hospital he would collect it again. No one would bother about it in the busy park; he'd pretend he'd lost the ticket for it when he checked out, so that no one would realize how long it had been there.

It was a nuisance, coming back by train. He had to change at Didcot, and there was a long wait with nothing to do. In the local train which took him to Felsbury he sat opposite two birds who had been looking him over on Didcot station. One had very long, skinny legs, and she waved her hands about a lot while she talked in an affected voice to her friend, all for Ray's benefit, he was sure. The other girl was plump and a bit spotty; he didn't fancy her. At Felsbury they both got out and he loitered behind them, waiting to see which way they would go. They parted at the bus-stop on the corner of City Road, and the long-legged one, with a toss of her mouse-coloured mane and a backward glance to make sure he was still there, set off on foot while her friend waited for the bus.

Ray went after the girl who was walking. She'd as good as said she was willing, by all her gestures. He didn't know where they could go; the night was cold.

There was always Friar's Alley, where few people came except those with the same idea. He'd been there often enough before.

'It was the same man?' asked Whitchurch. 'On Saturday?'

'Oh yes.'

Whitchurch forbore to point out that it was unfortunate Lorna had not reported this at once.

'And I saw him again. At least, I think it was. I'm not so certain about the next time.'

'And when was that?'

Purdy was right about the girl: she was an introverted type. In his impatience Whitchurch wanted to bark at her, but that would do no good. He waited.

'Yesterday. I was on my bicycle. It was near Diddington —where the road turns off, about four miles out of Felsbury.'

'Go on.'

'A car went by. I had to wait for it before I could cross the road. The man driving – it could have been the same one. I thought it was.'

'Hm. And what sort of a car was it?'

'I don't know. A small one – blue,' said Lorna.

'You didn't take the number?'

'No. I didn't realize at first – and then, I didn't know about Mrs Watson till today. If I had –' she stopped.

It was a good point. Whitchurch checked the place where this had happened with her on the map; the car was travelling away from Felsbury, she said, on the Bristol road. Purdy came back while they were establishing this, and Whitchurch sent her off with him to look at photographs of cars in the hope that she might recognize the one the man was driving.

But she could not do it. They let her go at last, warning her another time to come forward sooner.

'It's better to make a mistake, and for us to question the wrong man than for someone else to be attacked,' said Purdy sternly.

'Yes. I know. It wasn't that. I was busy,' Lorna said. 'I'm very sorry.'

'Funny sort of girl,' said Whitchurch when she had gone.

'Mm. Won't say she's sure of something unless she is,' said Purdy. 'That's sometimes a virtue.'

Monday had passed tranquilly for Ray. He continued normally with the delivery van, suffering the usual good-natured teasing from the women in the shop as he fetched the orders. He heard them discussing the attack on the woman from Floradora's; she was still in hospital, it seemed.

'Shocking,' said Ray, and to Rene, the older and fatter of the two women who had helped Mr Crawley for years, 'You want to be careful going home in the dark. Better wait for me to see you on your way.'

'Go on with you, Ray,' said Rene. 'I wouldn't be safe – you're such a one for the girls.'

Everyone giggled at this, and Ray thought, if they only knew.

He'd had a good time the night before. He and the girl from the train had gone down Dunstable Mews on the way to Friar's Alley, and there, in one of the backyards, he'd seen this big Humber; it was old, with a deep seat in the back. Better by far than standing out in the cold. It wasn't even locked. The girl turned out to be quite a one, well worth the effort. He hadn't arranged to meet her again, though; it was better to leave that to chance. She worked in Woolworth's so he knew where to find her. But he planned to quit in a few more days. After he'd done Mrs Malmesbury.

'All three victims came from within a few hundred yards of each other,' said Superintendent Whitchurch. 'The tea shop and the florist are in the same street, and the pub is just around the corner. What does that mean to you?'

'That the villain lives or works round there too,' said Purdy. 'Or he might be a regular punter. Lorna Gibson saw him outside the bookie's on Saturday.'

'He doesn't sound like the sort of character who'd hold down a steady job, somehow,' said Whitchurch. 'And nothing came of the enquiries we made after the girl first described him.'

'No. But we didn't do a door-to-door – just asked about discreetly, and everyone kept their eyes open. It was all a bit vague.'

'Hm. Well, the photo-fit is better now, since she got another look at him. Take it round to the bookie, Bob, and see if they recognize any of their regulars. And you might ask around more sharply than before. See who employs young chaps behind the counter, for instance. Send that young constable who's a snappy dresser – Frisby. He might spot him in one of the gent's outfitters. There are two along that way, aren't there?'

'Three, if you count Modern Man,' said Purdy. Poor Frisby: he would not enjoy this mission. He was a conventional young man with short back and sides, and a frank, open countenance. Modern Man sold unisex garments in a dim-lit cavern, with muzak. Well, it was all experience.

'We can't start until the morning, sir. There's no one there now.'

'No.' Whitchurch drummed his biro on the desk. His face, jowly and lined, wore a grim expression. 'That girl. Pity we couldn't get more out of her about the car. I wonder where he was going. He may have skipped.'

'What if I took her out and showed her actual vehicles?' suggested Purdy. 'We could look at them in parks. It might come back to her.'

'It can't do any harm, except waste your time. Why not send a constable?'

'She's an odd one. I think she's got some sort of confidence in me,' said Purdy. 'She might clam up with a copper she doesn't know. Especially a young one.'

'Going all psychological about her, are you?'

'You could say that,' said Purdy.

'Well, I suppose there's nothing else you're better doing, as things are,' said Whitchurch, and as he spoke there came a tap at the door. A constable entered.

'It's the hospital, sir,' he said. 'Mrs Watson died five minutes ago. She never regained consciousness.'

'Right,' snapped Whitchurch. 'Purdy, get that girl. show her every car in Felsbury if you have to. But find out what make it was. It's our only lead.'

'If it is one at all,' said Purdy.

Chapter 19

Purdy had to ring twice before Lorna came to the door.

'It's about that car, Miss Gibson,' he began at once. 'If I might come in.'

'Yes. All right.'

She'd been eating. A plate with traces of scrambled egg on it and a knife and fork, askew, was on the floor by the one armchair.

'I'm sorry, I've interrupted your meal,' he said.

'It's all right. I've finished.' Lorna picked up the plate and took it through to the sink.

Purdy heard running water and a clatter, then the pop of the gas. She was putting the kettle on. He glanced around. The room was just the same as on the two other occasions when he had been there. Then he noticed something dark poking out from under the bright bedspread that covered the divan. He went silently over to discover what it was and saw the corner of a knitted garment. Purdy tugged, and from under the pillow drew out a man's sweater, much worn and darned. St Michael size 40, said the label. He pushed it back quickly. Lorna herself could not be more than size 36; did she wear it at night? Or did it belong to a boyfriend? Or was it some sort of fetish?

He was standing by the empty wastepaper basket when Lorna appeared through the curtains.

'You'd like some tea,' she said.

Though it would waste time, he agreed; the few minutes it would take might be well used in getting her to relax.

'Do you cycle to work?' he asked.

'No, I go by bus,' she said. 'It's direct.'

It was probably warmer. He looked at her in her dark skirt and sweater, with her hair coiled neatly round her head, and tried to imagine her stretched out on a Spanish beach with her hair spread around her; he failed.

'So cycling's a hobby?'

'I suppose so.' It kept her fit, anyway; she was very wiry.

He told her then that Joyce had died.

Purdy drove Lorna round the town for nearly an hour. They went to the municipal park and walked past rows of cars whose owners were spending their Monday evening at the cinema, the pub, or various other spots. They stood at side roads and watched the passing traffic.

'It's dark now. It was daylight then,' said Lorna. 'I'm sorry to be so stupid. I don't know anything about cars. It was blue and small. That's all I know for certain.'

They eliminated Volkswagens. Lorna was sure she would have noticed the blunt nose and sloping back; or at least, she added carefully, she thought she would.

'No other car we've seen looks quite like that,' she said.

Purdy took her into a pub and bought her, without asking her what she wanted, a whisky and ginger ale.

'Now, forget about cars for a few minutes,' he said. 'We'll talk about something else and then try again. How long have you lived in Felsbury?'

She drank the whisky and told him. By degrees he got from her an outline of her childhood and adolescent years.

'So you've no family?'

'No. Oh, I'm quite happy,' Lorna said defiantly. 'I've got friends. Why, I was round at the Titmusses only the other night – he's the deputy librarian. And I had lunch in Diddington on Sunday. That's where I went on my bicycle. Mrs Guthrie asked me to lunch.'

It was all perfectly true.

'I keep busy,' she added.

Poor bitch, thought Purdy with compassion. He was not deceived.

When they left the pub he walked her round the corner and brought her up slap in front of the showroom of the biggest motor dealer in Felsbury. There was a blue Hillman Imp in the window. There were other small cars too, but she didn't even look at them.

'There it is. That's it!' she cried, and pointed at the Imp.

Purdy took her home then.

By midnight, all over the country, the police were alerted to question drivers of blue Imps about where they had been last Sunday afternoon. Purdy, driving back to his bachelor flat, could not put from his mind the two curious facts of the cut-out letters he had seen in Lorna's waste-paper basket on his first visit to her room, and the man's pullover under the pillow.

He wondered if the driver of the Hillman had recognized her, as they passed.

Ray heard the news of Joyce Watson's death when he got to the shop on Tuesday morning. Rene, Madge and Mr Crawley were all discussing it.

'Hanging's too good for the fellow that did it,' said Madge, her normally mild, plump face flushed with emotion.

'Why Ray, you've gone quite pale,' said Rene. 'It is a shock, isn't it?'

There was a small paragraph in the later editions of the daily papers, and it had been announced on the radio news.

'They'll not get him,' said Ray, rallying. 'He'll be far away by now.'

'Maybe,' said Madge.

They could not stand talking for long: the telephone rang and the first customer came into the shop. Ray went off to start the day's work.

Mrs Malmesbury went out most Tuesdays. He could go into her flat after she'd gone. But she'd be wearing her rings. Besides, in daylight someone might see him. No, he would have to wait till it was dark.

He took her order round as usual. She looked better today and had on a bright blue jumper which brought out the colour of even her faded old eyes. Round her neck was a string of pearls like you saw in Woolworth's, but in her case he'd bet they were real. He'd have that. He must just keep calm. There was nothing at all to link him with Mrs Watson.

With the radio on in the car, singing loudly as he drove along, Ray had never noticed Lorna on her bicycle.

After work on Tuesday, Lorna went over to The Lindens. The day at the surgery had been passed in a subdued atmosphere; even Nancy was shocked into silence by the murder so close to them. All day, Lorna had worked with icy detachment. She had made no mention of the car she had seen, and there had been nothing about the man she had described to the police on the one o'clock news, to which Nancy had listened on Mr Carruthers' portable radio. She supposed it might be reported in the evening paper.

June opened the door.

'I came to say how sorry I was to hear about Mrs Watson,' said Lorna carefully. 'What will you do at the shop?'

'We're carrying on. We got there this morning to find a whole load of flowers just dumped on the pavement outside – Joyce used to go in early.'

'You don't have to fetch them, then?'

'No. We've got agents who bring our orders. Of course, now she's dead, I suppose we'll have to close.' It was a new thought to June. 'We had felt we ought to keep going.'

'I see.'

'Come in a minute,' said June. She had been horrified by Joyce's death; in the shop they had been busy answering enquiries about her from shocked customers, as well as dealing with ordinary business; now reaction had set in. She could not discuss it with the children, and she welcomed the presence of another adult. 'There's a son in New Zealand. I suppose he'll decide what's to happen about the business,' she added.

Lorna stepped gratefully into the house. Cecil would be home soon. If she could prolong her visit she might see him. It wasn't yet time for June's weekly appointment: would she go tonight? Cecil might forbid it, in view of the killer prowling the streets of Felsbury. But if it was the man in the Imp, he must be far away by now.

The children greeted her with delight. Barty displayed the Nativity scene he had drawn at school, with a jumbo jet in flight over the Bethlehem stable. He leaned against Lorna while she admired this masterpiece, and surreptitiously she hugged him. Janet had spent much of the day learning about the habits of the honey bee, and she described them in painstaking detail.

'They must have their supper,' said June. 'I'm off soon to my Italian class. Pity you gave it up.'

'Yes.'

How could June do it? How could she lie like that? In the end, after helping to lay the table for supper, Lorna lost her nerve about waiting for Cecil and said she must go.

'Come again,' said June. She would keep in touch with Lorna. All sorts of ideas were in her mind about Floradora's. If the man from New Zealand wanted to keep it on, she could run it for him, but she would need more help: a girl like Lorna, mature and responsible, capable of turning her hand in any direction, not least towards Barty and Janet, might be vital to the success of such a venture.

Cecil arrived as she opened the door for Lorna.

'Lorna came to sympathize about Joyce. It was nice of her,' June said.

'Most thoughtful,' agreed Cecil. He looked tired.

He doesn't want to see me, Lorna thought. He wants to be alone with June. Well, alone with his family. I'm in the way.

'If I can do anything – help at all –' her voice trailed off.

'No one can now,' said Cecil grimly.

He was right, Lorna knew: it was too late for Joyce; but not too late to rescue Cecil.

Chapter 20

A leather holdall had been found in a yard behind the abattoir. It contained a woman's handbag, and papers that showed it belonged to Joyce Watson. There were several sets of prints, most of them blurred, though Mrs Watson's and the finder's came up clearly. There was another set, too.

'We've something here, anyway,' said Purdy studying these. 'But it's no one we know.'

'And young Frisby had no joy asking round the shops.'

'No.' But his instructions had been to use his own eyes, not the photofit. The police did not want to show their hand too soon.

'Hm. Well, go ahead now with the photofit. Put it out on television and in the press,' said the superintendent.

'Right, sir.' Now they might get somewhere. 'The switchboard's going mad with calls about blue Hillman Imps,' said Purdy. 'They've been seen all over Britain.'

'Good.'

'We're asking at all the local garages too,' Purdy added. 'I doubt if this character gets much maintenance done, though.'

'Probably doesn't insure his car either,' said Whitchurch. 'That is, if it is his, not one he's nicked.'

Tuesday was a busy day for Charlie. He'd had his ordinary booked-in repairs to do, plus an unexpected broken back axle. Then he'd been to the bank about the loan for the new garage. The interest was going to be crippling, but with Ted as his partner the future looked good. One or two hard years, and then they'd be away. Ted was a genius with engines; it was a pity he had this passion for driving around. Still, maybe he'd get over it. Meantime, Charlie would keep his ears open in case he heard of some reliable man wanting a driving job, another retired soldier, perhaps; someone older, who would rather spend his days in a comfortable car than in a draughty workshop.

All this was much on Charlie's mind when the policeman called to ask if he had serviced a blue Hillman Imp.

He did not service one regularly, and he forgot the one with the big end gone that he'd fixed a month or two back. It was only later, when he was in bed with Doreen, that he thought of it, and the young man who had paid the bill in fivers. Ted should be the one to tell the police about that, anyway, since he'd taken the money and made out the receipt.

It would be time enough in the morning.

When Ray got home late on Tuesday night, his mother was waiting up for him. He'd gone looking for Beverley, the girl from Woolworth's, but the store was closed when he got there. He hoped she might be in one of the cafés nearby, but there was no sign of her. He'd ended up in the back seat of the Regal with a bird who said she was eighteen, looked twenty-five, but was probably about fifteen. It passed the time. They went to the club, later, and he didn't leave her till after midnight.

His mother was in her dressing-gown, purple wool, it was, from Marks last Christmas; her pink brushed nylon nightdress showed below the hem; her hair was pinned up and moored under a thick net. Her eyes, pale blue like Ray's, were wide and anxious.

'Hullo, Mum. What you doing, then?' asked Ray. 'Dad out?'

His mother put a finger to her lips, adjuring silence.

'He's in bed. I said I'd to go to the toilet, when I heard you come in,' she said, in a whisper. 'Ray, you've to get out.'

'Get out? Why? What do you mean?'

'You done it, didn't you? That woman. There was a picture of you on the telly. It was you, Ray.'

'Come on, Mum! You're joking,' said Ray.

He tried to laugh, but a sick feeling caught him in the stomach.

'The police are looking for a young man to help with their enquiries. That's what it said,' his mother recited. 'That's what they always say. Then there was this picture of you, Ray. An identity kit one.'

'They're looking for the wrong bloke. I done nothing,' Ray began.

His mother went to the dresser and opened the drawer. From it she took a wad of money. His loot.

'I found it in your room, Ray. Under the floor. You get out now, while there's time. Before someone else recognizes you. Luckily it was on the late programme.'

He knew what she meant. If his brothers had seen it, they might have said, 'There's our Ray.'

'Did Dad see it?'

'He was asleep with the paper. I packed you a bag, and some sandwiches. Hurry, now.' There were tears in Mrs Brett's eyes.

'I didn't mean to hurt her badly, mum,' said Ray, and for a moment his features crumpled, as if he were a child.

'I know that, silly,' said Mrs Brett. 'It was an accident.' She pulled his head down roughly and deposited a brisk kiss on his cheek. 'Now go,' she said.

He paused only to collect the bag she had put ready, the money, and the food. Then he left.

Mrs Malmesbury heard a faint sound in the night. She slept lightly, and since Edgar died she had slept even less, often lying awake thinking of the past, and of her son, now so long dead, who would have been well into middle age now, if he had lived. How different things might have been. She would have had grandchildren, even great-grandchildren.

Since her illness her resilience had dwindled. She had spent only an hour in Felsbury with Ted this morning and had told him she would give up her weekly trip now winter had come. She would just go out occasionally, if there was a good film showing, or perhaps to Diddington for the day, if Hesther invited her. She would fit these things in when Ted was free and no longer tie him down to a regular time. Ted, in return, described the plan for the filling station; she thought it sounded excellent. It wouldn't be for a while yet, he told her. And even then, he'd always be available to drive her.

There it was again: a faint noise from the sitting-room. Never a coward, Mrs Malmesbury called out, 'Who's there?'

Ray, loading up silver ornaments and the late Colonel Malmesbury's medals into his zipped bag, cursed. He was wearing his stocking mask, but his voice gave him away when he came into Mrs Malmesbury's bedroom. She was sitting up in bed with the lamp on beside her, and a shawl dragged round her shoulders. Her skimpy white hair was on end, and she looked vulnerable even to Ray.

'Stay in bed, and no one won't hurt you,' he said.

'Ray Brett!' Shock, not fright, was in her voice.

Ray bent and pulled the telephone flex from the wall.

'Where's your rings?' he demanded.

Involuntarily, she looked at her dressing-table. Ray went to it. Her rings were in a leather case, with the pearls, a pair of ear-rings in some red stone that might have been rubies, and some brooches. He tipped the whole lot into a handkerchief which he tied in a knot and stowed away in his bag. Then he left the room, and Mrs Malmesbury heard him moving about.

She began to struggle out of bed. When he came back she was standing at the foot of the bed holding on to the bedpost, swaying.

'Sit in that chair,' he said, and pointed.

She looked like a real old crone in a long-sleeved nightdress which was the twin of his mother's.

'I – I can't,' she was going to say, for she thought that she could not get there unaided, without her stick. But soldier's widow that she was, she would not ask this thug for help. Tottering, dragging her thin bare feet over the carpet, she somehow did it, and collapsed into the button-backed chair with a small moan.

Ray had found twine in the kitchen; it was strong and thick, of the type used for clothes-lines before the plastic variety became popular. In the habit of elderly people not wanting to throw out things that might be useful, Mrs Malmesbury had stored it away. He lashed her firmly to the chair, with cords across her body, and with her thin old ankles tied to the legs in an inelegant posture.

'It's – it's cold,' she said, in a quavery voice, and to herself wondered why she did not scream. The answer was, she knew, because it would be so undignified.

As if he had read her mind, Ray rummaged through her drawers and pulled out a handful of scarves. He bound one firmly over her mouth; it bit into the flesh of her face. Then he strode to the door. On an impulse, once there, he looked back at his captive. She was shivering. He crossed to the bed and pulled off the eiderdown and top blanket. Roughly, he draped them around her, then went out, closing the door.

There were two policemen talking on the pavement

outside Cleveland Court when Ray crept stealthily down stairs. He did not use the lift in case he met someone in it.

He went straight back to Mrs Malmesbury's flat. Without turning on the light he crossed to the window; they were still down there, conferring, and as he watched a Panda car went past.

They would not look for him here. No one knew he had a key. He was safe enough, and the old trout, trussed as she was, could not possibly raise the alarm. His mother was not due till Friday, so he could lie up quite safely until then, if need be.

He went into the bedroom to look at his prisoner. The bedside light still burned: that was an oversight, for someone might wonder about it, seeing it on so late. Mrs Malmesbury's eyes stared at him above her gag. They were not frightened eyes, and he did not recognize the expression that was in them, for it was of an emotion alien to him: pity.

He snapped out the light. Somehow he could not stretch himself out on her bed while she remained bound to her chair. There was another bedroom in the flat, and he went to it, took the blanket from the bed, and spread himself out on the sofa in the sitting-room. Then he thought about having a drink; he could certainly do with one. He knew the old girl had plenty of booze, for he'd seen the bottles.

There was brandy in the sideboard. He carried the bottle over to the sofa, stretched out comfortably in front of the electric fire, and took a swig.

Soon, he slept.

Chapter 21

Lorna had studied the reports about Joyce Watson's death. She had been struck on the head by some object which had fractured the skull. It could have been a cosh, she supposed, whatever that was. What else did people get hit on the head with? She was not a reader of crime fiction, so was not informed about candlesticks, and lamps with heavy bases. Anyway, robbers didn't cart things like that around with them. Blunt instruments were what they used.

That was the way to do it: then the police would think it was all part of the same series of attacks, and the young man with the pale blue eyes would be blamed. He was already guilty of murder.

She startled Nancy by going out at lunch time on Wednesday saying she had some shopping to do, but when she returned she brought no parcels. Nancy looked at her in some concern. She had rings round her eyes and was even paler than usual.

'You all right, Lorna?' she asked. 'You look a bit done up.'

'I'm perfectly well, thanks.'

Nancy, who was loved by Joe, and who was therefore ready to love the whole world in return, even Lorna, gave her a pat on the arm, from which Lorna did not recoil.

'Come out on Saturday with Joe and me, Lorna. We'll get that friend of his, Norman, to come along. He's a nice fellow and good for a laugh. Do come. It'd cheer you up.'

By Saturday it would be over. She would do it tonight.

*

Apart from his mother, no one immediately connected Ray with the pictures on television and in the papers until he failed to report for work at Crawley's. Even then, it took Mr Crawley, Rene and Madge some time to put two and two together.

'Let's have another look at the paper,' said Rene, and they spread Mr Crawley's *Express* on the counter.

'It's like him,' said Crawley. 'Very like him.'

'But he was always such a nice lad. Always good for a joke,' said Rene.

Madge, his mother's friend, said nothing.

At last Mr Crawley rang up the police.

'It's for them to judge,' he pronounced.

Detective Chief Inspector Purdy came round very quickly, bringing a fingerprint expert. It was not long before they established that prints in Crawley's van matched those on the purse found in Joyce Watson's holdall.

'He'll be miles away by now,' said Purdy.

But they went straight round to the Bretts' flat.

How long before Ted came back, wondered Lorna.

She stood in the darkness of Dunstable Mews. The yard where Ted parked the big car was empty; so was the garage, whose doors stood open.

He might be away for hours, she supposed, and shivered. It was drizzling slightly, and she had pulled her anorak hood over her head. Her hands were thrust into the deep pockets. One or two cars passed, but no one saw her in her shadowy spot behind the gate.

Ted might close it when he came back, and find her there.

She would run away, if he did. He'd be surprised, and

she'd be swift enough to grab her bike and be gone before he could catch her.

After a long time a pair of headlights moved slowly up the narrow road, slewed round, and the Humber turned in. Ted got straight out and went up the stairs to his room. Lorna sighed. He'd stay there. It was so cold and wet that no one would want to come out unless they must.

She crept into the yard, closer to the car. If her opportunity did not come tonight, then she must try tomorrow. This was the only way to help Cecil; no one else could take June's place.

It began to rain harder. Lorna hesitated, then tried the car door nearest to her. It was unlocked, and she got in, crouching down on the floor of the rear.

Quite soon, she heard Ted's approaching feet, and her heart raced. He opened the door in front of her.

Lorna's grip tightened around the heavy-headed hammer she had bought during her lunch-hour and had hidden, this evening, up the sleeve of her anorak. She took a deep breath, raised herself into a kneeling position and struck the head of the man who had just got into the car. He groaned and the car's horn blared as he slumped against the wheel. Lorna hit out blindly again. Ted's body moved, and the terrible noise of the horn ceased.

She could feel something wet and warm on her hands.

He must be dead.

Lorna scrambled from the car and ran, flinging the hammer away as she rushed out of the alley.

Early on Wednesday morning a blue Hillman Imp had been found among the few cars still left in a multi-storey park in Bristol. There was a wilted chrysanthemum on the floor, and when the police opened the boot they discovered a black leather bank bag with its lock broken.

'So he has left our patch,' said Purdy, later that day.

'Looks like it,' said Superintendent Whitchurch.

'He may have hopped aboard a ship by now,' Purdy remarked.

He had not enjoyed his interview with Mrs Brett. She had denied all knowledge of Ray's whereabouts, but one of the younger children, not at school because he had a stomach upset, had let out that he'd seen his brother with 'something funny' over his face once. They'd gone over his room very thoroughly and found the loose floorboard, though there was nothing beneath it now.

In the evening Purdy went round to tell Lorna that the man she had seen had been identified, and that the car had been found. Without television, she might not have followed the progress of the search. But there was no answer when he rang her bell and, after waiting a while, he gave up.

Somehow Ted dragged himself out of the car and stumbled across the yard to the steps. Blood streamed down the side of his head, and his legs kept buckling under him. He did not know how long he had been unconscious. He managed to stagger towards the staircase; if he could reach the telephone, help would come

Clutching the banister rail, he began to climb. It was raining hard, and the wooden steps were slippery. He was almost at the top, on the point of reaching out for the doorhandle, when his foot slipped; his precarious balance was lost and he pitched backwards, unable to save himself, carried on by his own bulk till he hit the stones at the foot of the stairway and lay spreadeagled on the ground.

The rain beat down, but Ted did not move.

Ray took Mrs Malmesbury's portable radio into the

kitchen on Wednesday morning and listened to the news while he cooked himself eggs and bacon. He heard the announcer say that Ray Brett, aged twenty, was wanted to help the police with their enquiries into the attack on Mrs Joyce Watson which had resulted in her death. The blue Hillman Imp thought to be connected with the case had been found in Bristol.

It gave him a thrill to hear himself mentioned like that on the air.

But he'd get away. He'd dye his hair to start with. That would be a good disguise. But he daren't risk slipping round to the chemist for a bottle of stuff, and this old bag wasn't the sort to have any. Still, she might have something that would do temporarily – bootblack, for instance. She'd bought shoe-polish from Crawley's; although his mother had told her that neutral cream was best for all shoes, she'd stuck to her Cherry Blossom. He'd try it. He'd got the whole day to occupy, after all.

As an afterthought, he poured out a cup of tea for Mrs Malmesbury, and took it and two digestive biscuits into the bedroom. He stood over her while she was briefly ungagged and fed her the biscuits, broken up, as you would to a child, and held the cup to her lips, though without any gentleness. All the time her eyes watched him, with that look they'd had the night before, that he could not understand. She dribbled a bit, and had some trouble eating the biscuits, though he didn't know why for she seemed to have plenty of teeth; he'd seen just a few on a plate in the bathroom. He had thrown it on the floor and stood on it, crushing it under his heel.

Her newspaper arrived through her letter-box, and a bottle of milk was outside the door when he looked out to see if there was anyone about. There were sounds from other parts of the building, but he saw no one.

For lunch he opened a tin of stewed steak, and another of peaches. He gave the old girl more tea and biscuits.

While she was ungagged she asked to go to the lavatory. She seemed to have difficulty in speaking.

Against his will, he allowed her to go, and she demanded her stick. He armed himself with the poker and followed her to the door, which must, he said, be left open. She stood there looking at him, without attempting to use the facilities, until at last he moved away, out of range of that unflinching stare.

When she had done, she walked back to her bedroom and wrapped the blanket and eiderdown right round herself before sitting down to be tied up again. She did not speak.

In the afternoon Ray watched racing on television. It was warm and comfortable, and he felt no fear. He would get away; they'd be looking for him in Bristol.

He had a go at his hair when the racing ended. It was rather a messy job with the boot-polish; he spread it on a brush and then worked it in. The result was not perfect but it would do. At ten o'clock he left the flat. He did not want to be on the streets too late, when he might attract attention with few pedestrians about, and he wanted to pick up a car. He might find one unlocked outside a pub. It was quite by chance that he turned down Dunstable Mews and remembered the Humber.

It was there, out in the yard, as it had been on Sunday night, and the key was in the dash. Ray backed it out, turned around, and headed towards London. Anywhere but Bristol.

The blood was everywhere: all over her anorak sleeve, down her arm, even a streak on her face where she had rubbed it. Lorna stared at it in the mirror, horrified. She dragged off her anorak and bundled it into a paper carrier; she'd put it out in the dustbin with the rubbish. Her other clothes she put into the polythene bag she used for the launderette; then she had a bath. By that time it was after eleven, but she went out to the launderette; she would not feel clean until she had removed all traces of blood from her body and possessions.

The launderette closed at midnight. She sat there, alone except for one fat old woman, while her clothes whirled round. She had not thought beyond this point. The thing was done: Cecil was no longer threatened.

When she got home her hair was soaked with the rain that had not stopped falling since she left Dunstable Mews; without her anorak, her sweater was wet too. She rubbed her hair with a towel and got undressed. Then, holding Cecil's old sweater close to her, much as Barty hugged his giraffe, she waited for sleep.

Oddly enough, it came at once; she had the best night she had known for a week.

Sightings of Ray Brett were being reported from all over England by the next morning. Each had to be followed up; it might be the right one.

At nine o'clock a Mrs Ford from Diddington, hitherto unknown to them, rang Felsbury central police station. She was concerned because she had tried several times to telephone her friend Mrs Malmesbury the day before but the number perpetually gave the engaged signal.

'Why doesn't she report it to the exchange?' said the sergeant at the desk. 'It must be out of order. Tell her to.'

'She has. But she's worried. Mrs Malmesbury is elderly and had recently been ill,' relayed the constable who took the call.

'Right. Tell her we'll send someone round,' said the sergeant.

*

The milkman found Ted.

The body was lying, sodden, at the foot of the stairway, and after his first shock abated, the milkman went up to see if the door was unlocked. He could tell at once that Ted was dead, so he rang the police; it was too late for any ambulance. He waited in his van till they arrived.

Purdy and his sergeant followed on the heels of the squad car that was first to reach Dunstable Mews. The rain had stopped, but there were puddles in the hollows of the cobblestones and in the gutters by the road's edge. Ted's gaberdine raincoat and his dark trousers were soaked.

'Who was he?' Purdy asked the milkman.

'Name of Ted Jessop. Runs a hire car,' said the milkman.

'I knew him, sir,' said one of the constables. 'He was a nice chap. Doing all right too.'

'Hm,' said Purdy. 'Right. Get on with it.'

He went up the stairs into Ted's room while the routine began below. It was all very neat, but stark; there were no concessions to comfort. A few books stood on a shelf, some paperbacked novels and three or four hardbacks about motor mechanics. There was a diary beside the telephone. Entered for the evening before was a trip to the station at eight forty-five. On Tuesday evening a line was drawn through the booking period from six-forty-five till nine-fifteen. Purdy riffled through the pages and saw that the same time was scored out on other Tuesdays.

'Hm,' said Purdy, reading on. 'Hullo, Mrs Malmesbury at eleven o'clock on Tuesday morning – here – and here – now why do I know that name?'

'There was a call just before we got this one, sir,' said his sergeant. 'Something about a Mrs Malmesbury's phone being out of order.'

Purdy nodded. He opened a drawer at the table. There were notebooks inside, a bank paying-in book, some bill forms and a packet of cheap envelopes. And a scarf, a woman's headscarf, blue and yellow.

The doctor had come, and Purdy went back down the stairs leaving the scarf where it was. The wooden steps were mossy in spots, and very slippery.

'Blow on the head,' said the doctor briefly. 'Rain's washed away a lot of the blood, though. Not hard enough to kill. He's broken his neck. Can't tell you more till we get at him properly.'

Purdy shuddered inwardly at the phrasing. Sudden death still sickened him. One got used to it, but one's sensibilities must remain aware. However, Dr Hodge was, he knew, a humane man, even if he did use blunt language.

'Where's this fellow's car?' asked Purdy suddenly. He looked round at the milkman, who was still there. 'You say he was a hire-car driver. What sort of car did he have? Where did he keep it?'

'Yonder, in the garage,' said the milkman. 'I've seen it often, he loved it, polished it like a baby, he did,' he added, with a fine disregard for metaphor. 'A black Humber – a big old one, you know.'

They looked at the garage. Its doors stood wide and it was empty.

It was at this point that a radio message came in to say that Mrs Malmesbury had been tied up and gagged in her flat by Ray Brett, for whom a large part of the British police force was now looking.

Chapter 22

In the morning, Lorna realized that she had forgotten to take Ted's wallet. Her plan had been so vague: all that was clear was the intention to hit him in the same manner that Ray Brett had hit Joyce Watson, then indicate robbery as the motive by taking what money she could find. But panic had taken over: to hit someone like that, a man she did not know and had seen only a few times, was a frightful thing to do, even if she meant only to put him out of action, not to kill him. She was not sure herself how far she meant to go.

She felt calm as she set off for work. On the way, she threw her anorak in its paper carrier into the dustbin. It did not occur to her to worry that it might be found and the bloodstains investigated; she wanted only to be rid of it. No one would connect her with what had happened to Ted; Ray Brett would be blamed.

All morning she worked calmly, and was once more efficient.

'They haven't caught that Ray Brett yet,' said Nancy as she put on her coat at lunch time. She was meeting Joe and was in a hurry. 'Makes you shudder, doesn't it?'

'They'll get him, I expect,' said Lorna, but she did not really care. Later events were more important to her than what Ray had really done.

'Bye, then,' said Nancy, and flew off down the stairs, legs flashing in new suede boots.

Lorna had forgotten to buy bread the day before, so she had brought no lunch, but there were biscuits in the office.

She ate three custard creams and drank two cups of tea.

Just before two, Vigors and Nancy arrived back together and met outside the surgery, Vigors parking his Volvo while Nancy stood on the corner staring down the road.

'What's going on, Nancy?' asked Vigors.

'There's a police car over the way, at that house round the corner. I wondered what was up,' she said.

'Probably a parking offence,' said Vigors. 'Most crimes are petty ones.'

'You're right, I suppose,' said Nancy.

She told Lorna about the police car, however.

Ted's wallet lay on Purdy's desk. The contents were spread about: twenty-three pounds in notes, his driving licence, an Access card, some of his own business cards. And a newspaper cutting.

Purdy stared at it. It was a photograph of a woman in evening dress with her hair drawn up to the top of her head, then falling below her ears. The figure had obviously been cut from a group: part of someone else's dress showed on one side of it.

'I know her. Who is she?' said Purdy, dredging his memory. 'She didn't look like this when I saw her, though.'

'It's that Mrs Titmuss,' said the sergeant.

Black sweater and jeans, and long, tawny hair; yes, it was the same face.

'Check with the *Gazette*,' said Purdy. 'I'm going round to the hospital. If that is Mrs Titmuss, we'll see her straight afterwards.'

Mrs Malmesbury was dozing when he got there. A policewoman sat outside the door of her side ward.

'How is she?' Purdy asked the staff nurse.

'Very weak,' said the nurse.

184

Mrs Malmesbury stirred when they came into her room. She felt very tired, but the ordeal was over. She could talk. The most dreadful thing about it all was the wet chair. There had been no alternative. Somehow she'd managed, that first day, to hold on until the boy let her go to the bathroom; stiff as she was, after being tied up all those hours, she'd got there alone, too, without falling, or needing his aid. But after he left, in the end there was nothing to be done. She would never forget the humiliation, nor the look on the face of the young policeman as he cut her free. She had never wanted pity; she did not want it now.

Hesther was responsible for her rescue, she learned; but for her she might not have been found until Mrs Brett arrived on Friday.

Mrs Brett: poor, well-intentioned woman whose son had done this cruel thing.

She told the inspector about it; times were rather a blur but she did her best to be clear.

She did not know when Ray had left, but he'd had the television on, turned to the commercial programme, for she had heard the advertisement jingles at intervals. She had not heard the news, so he must have left before ten.

'I was quite surprised that he bothered to turn it off,' she said to Purdy. 'Will you catch him? I don't want to make too much fuss, but he must be punished. And I would like my rings back.'

'He didn't just rob you, Mrs Malmesbury,' said Purdy gently. 'We want him for another matter.' He stood up. 'Don't worry about it now. You rest. I'm sure you'll soon feel better.'

'Yes.' She closed her eyes. 'Yes, I will.'

She was safe now. There was nothing more to fear.

June went to the shop as usual that morning, but they

closed for the afternoon because of the inquest on Joyce. When she got home and found a police car outside the house, she was not alarmed. It was about the inquest, due to start at three, she supposed.

The same youngish man in plain clothes who had come before got out of the car as she walked up to the house from the bus-stop. He had a square jaw and a rugged look, in a way rather like Ted.

'I'd like a word, Mrs Titmuss, please,' he said.

'Of course.'

June set down her basket and searched for her key in her handbag. Unlike Cecil, she was not always orderly, and it took some finding among the clutter.

Purdy watched her hunt. She was in for a shock. He had pity for Ted, and he reserved his feeling for June. He did not know yet what she merited.

June found the key at last and opened the door. She took him into the dining-room. It was much lived-in, he saw, unlike the sitting-room where he had been on his other visit. There were books on a desk, papers on the table, and a half-finished model of a matchstick building which Purdy had no difficulty in recognizing.

'It's Notre Dame,' he exclaimed.

'Yes. How clever of you.'

'It couldn't be anything else. How marvellous!' He bent to look at it. 'Who's doing this? Not your children, surely?'

'Goodness, no. It's my husband. He likes this sort of thing. It's his hobby.'

'He must have plenty of patience.' Purdy found the work impressive.

'Oh, he has,' said June. 'He's done several others just as complicated. Well,' she looked at him. 'Won't you sit down?'

'Thanks,' said Purdy.

She was very poised, regarding him calmly.

'Would you like some sherry?' she asked, crossing to the sideboard.

'Not on duty, thanks,' said Purdy. 'But don't let me stop you.'

She picked up some papers that lay on the sideboard and put them in a drawer.

'My latest competition,' she said. 'I can't resist them. Cornflake packets, and things, you know.'

'Have you ever won anything?'

'A camera,' she said. 'Not a car, or anything exciting. I suppose you've come about the inquest.'

'Well, not exactly,' said Purdy. 'Do you know a Ted Jessop, of 57 Dunstable Mews?'

She might not. He could be a nut, carrying round her photograph, and the scarf might have belonged to anyone, a passenger in his car. But a long, tawny hair had been found in Ted's bed. And other traces. It would be awkward, if she wouldn't admit it and they had to be matched. But there'd be her hairbrush, for a start.

She did not answer at once.

'I – er – I've met him,' she said at last.

She took a sherry glass from the sideboard and filled it from the bottle. Her hand was steady. Then she turned. Against the window, her face was shadowed.

'I should come and sit down, Mrs Titmuss,' Purdy said.

June obeyed. What could this mean? Had Ted been carrying on with Joyce too? Surely not.

'Ted Jessop was found dead this morning,' said Purdy. It was the only way to do it: you couldn't build up gradually to this kind of revelation, and he wanted her spontaneous reaction.

She gave a gasp and dropped the sherry glass, which spilled its contents on the floor and on her skirt.

Purdy produced a large clean handkerchief and gave it to her. She mopped herself up, her face white. She had not said a word.

'It won't stain,' said Purdy, dabbing at the carpet when she had handed back the handkerchief.

'An accident? The car?' she said at last.

At least she was not hysterical.

'He was hit over the head with a blunt instrument,' said Purdy promptly.

'Oh God! You mean he was murdered?' She put her face in her hands at this, but she did not weep.

Purdy knew that the blow had not killed Ted; he had died of the fall he had sustained later, but the cause of that fall was uncertain: he might have been pushed, or it might have been an accident. Either way, he would not reveal the details. He went over to the sideboard and looked in it. There was a bottle of whisky nearly empty. He poured what was left into the glass that had held the sherry and gave it to June.

'I should drink this, Mrs Titmuss,' he said, and stood over her as she obeyed.

'That man – that Ray Brett you're supposed to be looking for – it was him, wasn't it?' said June.

'It looks like it. The car's gone – Jessop's car. He may have caught Brett stealing it.'

'Why are you here?' June said. 'How did you know I knew him?'

Purdy took a plastic folder from his pocket and showed her the newspaper cutting. He took the scarf out too.

'Is this yours?'

June nodded.

Purdy replaced it.

'I must keep it for the moment,' he said.

'Where did you find the photograph?'

'In his wallet.'

June looked at it, and two tears slid slowly down her face. Purdy watched, fascinated. He had heard about women who could weep without losing their beauty, and here was one doing it. He had never seen it happen before.

'I can't help you,' she said.

'Were you having an affair?' asked Purdy in an even voice.

She did not protest.

'You seem to have guessed.'

'Does your husband know?'

'Good heavens, of course not! No one knew,' cried June.

'How long had it been going on?'

She told him about their Tuesdays.

'Your husband didn't suspect?'

'You've met him,' June said. 'Do you think he would?'

'You were taking a risk. He might have come to the college to meet you.'

'He had to stay here with the children,' said June. 'It was perfectly safe.'

'He might have met your tutor and asked how you were getting on.'

June stared.

'Did he?' she asked.

'I don't know,' said Purdy. 'But I shall find out.'

Chapter 23

When the surgery closed, Lorna went over to The Lindens. She must find out why the police had called there. It was Thursday, so Cecil would be working late.

'I mustn't stop. I just wondered how you all are,' said Lorna, when June opened the door.

Despite her own troubles, June recognized that Lorna seemed to be under some strain.

'We're fine. Janet's doing her homework and Barty's cutting the heads off matches for Cecil. Come in and have a cup of tea,' she said.

She was glad to see Lorna; if she did not talk to some adult soon, she would explode.

'The police were here this morning,' she said in a bright voice, filling up the kettle. 'It was really about the inquest on Joyce. I didn't have to go. They said it would be adjourned. But they told me that man has killed somebody else. A taxi driver. And taken his car.'

'His car?'

'Yes. He was hit over the head, like Joyce, and his car has gone.'

But she had left him in the car; he was slumped over the wheel and his blood was all over her. What did it mean?

'He'll be far away by this time,' June said. 'That Ray Brett.'

'I suppose so,' said Lorna, utterly bewildered.

'I wonder if they'll get him,' said June. 'They usually do, when it's this sort of thing.'

'Yes.'

They drank their tea and discussed the affair for half an hour, in the comfort of June's kitchen. Then Lorna left.

She went straight to the library, her mind in tumult.

Cecil was in his usual place, behind his glass wall. Lorna sat in the reference section watching him, pretending to read a magazine. She was still there when Detective Chief Inspector Purdy came into the library and walked straight through into the office.

'You should have told him,' said Whitchurch.

'I couldn't do it,' Purdy answered.

'It wouldn't be news to him. He knows already. Of course he does. Young Brett didn't kill Jessop. There were none of his prints in the flat or on that hammer, yet they were all over the bag we found,' said the superintendent.

For a constable had found the hammer which Lorna had flung from her; there were faint prints on the handle, and traces of Ted's hair on the head although the rain had washed most of the blood away.

'He doesn't know, and I couldn't tell him,' said Purdy.

'What's got into you, Bob? You're getting soft,' said Whitchurch. 'Good God, man, it's obvious.'

'It's not. Titmuss wouldn't hurt a fly,' said Purdy.

'Come off it, Bob. You fancy the wife – all right – that doesn't let her husband off the hook. You know as well as I do that those meek ones can be violent when they're pushed.'

'Not Titmuss,' said Purdy. 'He really thought she was at her Italian lessons each Tuesday.'

'How did you find out?'

'Said I wanted to know the names of some tutors, and if he could tell me it would save me ringing the college and getting no further, since at that time of the evening the office would be closed.'

'And?'

'He didn't know. Consulted some list or other, which didn't say, and then rang the principal at his home.'

'Clever bugger,' said Whitchurch. 'And more fool you, Purdy.'

'I got prints,' said Purdy. 'Nicked a biro off his desk. He'd just put it down.'

'Well, we can see if he went to Jessop's place, then. Except that he'd have had the sense to wear gloves. What about hers? Mrs Titmuss? Did you get them?'

'No. She was too upset,' said Purdy.

'You were, you mean. Really, Purdy, the girl's a looker – maybe. But you're a copper. And a good one.'

'I think Brett took the car,' said Purdy. 'He'd dumped his own, remember. He may have known about Jessop from Mrs Malmesbury, and gone round there on the off chance. It's not so far from Cleveland Court.'

'Too much of a coincidence,' said Whitchurch.

'Well, if Titmuss attacked Jessop, why did he take the car, and where is it now?' demanded Purdy. 'No. Brett did this. Maybe Jessop caught him taking the car or maybe Brett clobbered him to get at the keys, but he did it.'

'Well, you haven't convinced me. I believe this mild man you describe, Titmuss, found out his wife was having it off with the fellow, did him, then took the car to make it look as if Brett was responsible. We'll find that Humber not far away, pretty soon. Being this meek chap you think he is, Titmuss didn't make a job of it with the hammer, and Jessop came round, staggered about a bit, and then fell. In fact the attack may have taken place at the top of those wooden stairs. He may have opened the door to his attacker.'

'Whoever hit him did it from behind,' said Purdy. 'That's what the doctor said.'

'If it was Titmuss, what more likely than that Jessop should ask him in, and turn his back to lead the way?'

It was all possible.

'There's no proof,' said Purdy.

'You're going to find it,' said the superintendent.

The library closed soon after Purdy's visit. Cecil went into the staff park and got into the car. He undid the lock on the steering column and laid the rod in its place under the dash. Then he started the engine, allowing it to warm up before moving away.

It was raining again; his windscreen wipers sighed back and forth. It would·be nice to get home. Such terrible things were happening all over the world, and now horror had come to Felsbury. He remembered the taxi-driver who had been killed from when Mrs Malmesbury collapsed in the library. And she, too, had been the victim of a cruel assault. Imagine, at her age, being tied to a chair for twenty-four hours by a young thug. What made a young man do such things?

It must be he who had killed Ted Jessop. It was to be hoped the police caught him before he attacked someone else.

Cecil drove on. He might be able to finish another flying buttress tonight.

It was odd that Detective Chief Inspector Purdy had elected to ask at the library about the names of the evening class tutors. Why did he want to know them? Surely it could have waited till morning, when the college secretary would have supplied the answer. He'd asked about several, including the one who taught Italian. Of course, it was just chance that he, Cecil, had been on duty when he called.

Cecil did not know that Purdy had learned from June that this was his late night at the library. He knew very little about the circumstances of Jessop's death, just what he had heard mentioned during the day, and the brief report in the evening paper.

June had made goulash, and Cecil ate with enjoyment though it was rather spicy; he hoped she had not included too many blood-heating ingredients. She liked what he called fancy cooking. Cecil himself inclined more and more towards nature foods, and sprinkled wheat germ each day on his breakfast cereal.

June was looking rather pale; she ate very little goulash.

'The police came to the library this evening,' he told her, finishing his caramel custard. It was rather too sweet.

'Oh? Why? What did they want?'

'The names of various evening class tutors. Yours among them. They didn't say why.'

June stared at him.

'Did you know who they were?'

'No, but I found out by ringing the principal. You'd have thought the police could have done that themselves.'

'Yes, wouldn't you?' she agreed, outwardly calm. But her heart was thudding and she felt rather sick.

Cecil turned on the television in time for the news. There were the usual troubles about oil and Northern Ireland, and then, there on the screen, was Detective Chief Inspector Purdy talking about the Felsbury murders. The police were looking, he said, for the young man, Ray Brett, who it was hoped could help them in their enquiries, and for the black Humber car. It was not certain, though, that the two deaths were connected and another line was being followed concerning the attack on Ted Jessop. Then they showed a snapshot of Ted, in army uniform, taken some years before. June's stomach turned over at the sight of it. She made some mumbled excuse and went upstairs.

Cecil liked being alone, but with the knowledge that the rest of the family were safe at home. He assembled his glue and the knife for his model. A heap of neatly decapitated matchsticks lay ready for him, after Barty's labours. June insisted that it was safe to let the child do this job, though

Cecil dreaded a mutilated finger. While he worked, he turned over in his mind what he had just heard. That man, the driver, was an ordinary, decent citizen. So was Joyce, a harmless woman with no known enemies. It was dreadful that they should be the victims of violence. And if Brett had not killed Jessop, then who had?

And why did the police want to know about the Tuesday tutors? For it had been Tuesday that interested Purdy. Jessop was killed on a Wednesday. So a Tuesday tutor could have done it, if he'd had cause. What cause? Cecil's mind ground slowly round. Ted had not, it seemed, been robbed.

June came back into the room. She looked as if she had been crying.

Cecil set a matchstick in place with a careful hand.

'What is the name of your Italian tutor?' he asked.

'He was dead keen on this bird,' said Charlie. 'Kept very quiet about it. Married, of course. Poor bastard, I still can't believe it.'

He was in his workshop with Purdy and the sergeant. All were drinking strong tea from enamel mugs. He'd already told Purdy what he could about Ted as soon as he heard the news, but not about the woman. That had nothing to do with the matter, he'd thought.

But it had, so they seemed to think.

Burton, the undertaker, had rung up Charlie early that morning in a fury. Ted hadn't turned up for a funeral booking and there was no reply to the phone. Charlie had gone round to the mews, arriving soon after the police.

'Who did it? This Brett character?' asked Charlie.

'Maybe.' Purdy was guarded. 'We'll know more when we find the car.'

'You think it might be this bird's husband?' Charlie pounced.

'We'll know soon enough,' said Purdy.

'You could be right,' said Charlie slowly. 'Ted wasn't so bright, these last few days. He'd been a carefree sort of bloke, you know. But not lately.' He told Purdy about their joint plans for the future. All that might go west now, without Ted's stake. Still, that was by the way. 'But Ted was a nice chap, Inspector. Never hurt anyone.'

'He was hurting this woman's husband,' said Purdy.

'Depends how you look at it. She was the one doing the hurting, I'd say, being a party to carrying on with Ted. And who's to say why she did that? Maybe her husband was the cause of it all.'

Who, indeed, was to say?

Chapter 24

Next day, during a gap in the morning's work at Floradora's, June read the newspaper report of Ted's death. Tracy could think of little else but the dreadful events that had happened one after the other in the town.

'I wonder who he was carrying on with?' she asked. 'It might have been someone we know – a customer.'

Her paper carried a headline: WHO WAS THE SECRET MISTRESS? June, heart plummeting, borrowed it and read the story. A persistent reporter had winkled Charlie out and somehow provoked a remark that had led to speculation about Ted's love life.

Well, the police knew the woman's identity. With resignation June accepted the fact that her own involvement was almost certain to be revealed. She had fobbed Cecil off about the tutor, saying that no one ever used her name and she'd never enquired what it was. She was able to describe the teacher convincingly, for she had, after all, attended two classes. Cecil had seemed satisfied and had continued with his model, just as usual. She had pleaded a headache and gone to bed, then feigned sleep when he came up later. That part was easy.

Only three nights ago she had been in Ted's arms. Now all that urgency had been extinguished. It was unbelievable. She thought of him less as a person than as the owner of a vigorous body; there had never been time to wonder what he thought about, apart from her.

Was it a crime of passion? demanded Tracy's paper, and went on to enquire if a jealous husband or lover had sought Ted out and killed him.

It couldn't be that.

Cecil could never have found out. Such an idea would never cross his mind. Even if, accepting the impossible, he had discovered, he would have taken it calmly—been sad, even angry, but not savage. In fact, his very lack of savagery was one of the things that June deplored about him. This was a typical example of a newspaper starting a theory to boost sales, June told herself. If the police had been thinking along those lines Inspector Purdy would have said so, or at least given a hint.

It was all horrible, though; like some nightmare.

When Peter Guthrie telephoned to say he was in town for the day and had just been to the library where her husband had most helpfully found him a book about tank design, and would she have lunch with him, she accepted at once.

'I'm sure you need your mind taken off this terrible business,' he said.

It took June a moment or two to realize that he was referring to Joyce's death, not Ted's.

Nancy, as always, was well informed.

'You remember him, don't you? The fellow that used to drive Mrs Malmesbury? 'Course, I wasn't here the last time she came, but I remember him all right. Nice-looking chap, he was. He'd a way with him.'

'Oh – is that who it was?' said Lorna. She must imply that she had no idea who Ted Jessop was.

'Lorna, don't you take anything in?' asked Nancy. 'Don't you notice anything? What are you doing with your eyes all the time?' Nancy took a keen interest in the doings of her neighbours and had a genuine liking for humanity. No one had ever been really unkind to her in all her twenty-four years. 'You'll be telling me next you only know Mrs Malmesbury as a name in the files.'

'No, I remember her all right,' said Lorna.

'Poor old thing. Tied up like that all night. It's a wonder she didn't die of it,' Nancy said. 'Now, Lorna, you're coming out with Joe and me tomorrow night. That's settled. You need to get out more. Norman's looking forward to meeting you.' He wasn't, but he had no other fish to fry at the moment and Nancy said it was all in a good cause. 'Besides, you never know, she might turn out to be your type in the end,' she had added optimistically.

'I don't think –' Lorna began.

'Well, I do,' interrupted Nancy, and then, with total irrelevance, 'I wonder if it was the husband?'

'What husband?'

Nancy had brought her lunch to the office today as it was raining. She was toasting a muffin, which she would spread with peanut butter.

'The mystery woman's,' said Nancy, and then explained, 'Ted Jessop had a mistress, a married woman. The police think her husband may have killed him from jealousy, not that Ray Brett at all.'

Lorna felt sick. A real pain hit her stomach and she thought she would vomit.

Nancy, busy toasting, did not notice.

'Some man he was going to open a garage with knew about her,' she went on. 'The paper didn't say who she is, but I bet the police know by now.'

Detective Chief Inspector Purdy had called at the library the evening before. But he had left alone, not taking Cecil with him. He had been to The Lindens too, though June had said his visit was about Joyce Watson. But then, she'd been so cool about Ted, as if his death meant nothing to her. How could she act so calmly?

Lorna could eat no more of her cheese sandwich.

Cecil had read the papers too. The *Guardian*, which he

read at breakfast, was not much interested in events in Felsbury, but the chief librarian's secretary had brought in the *Daily Mail*. When she was out of the office on an errand Cecil read the whole story. She came back to find him immersed.

'Terrible, isn't it, Mr Titmuss?' said the girl.

'Indeed it is. I'm so sorry, Miss Vernon – I hope you didn't mind. The headline caught my attention.'

'Not at all, Mr Titmuss.'

He was always so polite. The chief librarian was sometimes peremptory, but never Mr Titmuss.

Throughout the morning Cecil carried on normally with his work. He spent nearly an hour with Peter Guthrie who came searching for books about early tanks. At lunch-time he went round the corner to The Salad Bowl as usual, where he ate lettuce with dates and cheese and drank a glass of mild.

Various thoughts circled round in his mind.

The name of the Italian tutor.

Ted Jessop had a married mistress.

June was behaving oddly; she had been disturbed the night before and had been vague this morning. It was too long after the event to pin this on shock from Joyce Watson's death.

It seemed that if Ted Jessop had not been killed by Ray Brett, he had been killed by a jealous husband. He, Cecil, had not killed Ted Jessop, therefore if that theory was correct some other man had done it, and that other man's wife was Jessop's mistress. Not June.

How could he ever entertain the idea that June even knew Ted Jessop, much less was his mistress? She had never met him.

But on Tuesdays she always returned radiant from her Italian classes. He had supposed it was the stimulus of the lessons.

He rang her at two, but Tracy said she was not yet back

from lunch. He was surprised; he thought she had taken sandwiches. Since Joyce's death she had stayed at the shop till the children came out of school.

For the first time ever, he left the library early and went home by way of the technical college. There, a young woman in the office recognized him, and this helped with his query. He had thought it up during the afternoon, and now said that he wanted to know which were the most popular evening classes; it might affect library buying, he explained.

Obligingly, she ran through the register. He asked if attendance had dropped for many subjects; people's enthusiasm wore off, he knew, as the winter advanced.

Over her shoulder he could see the ticks on the Italian register: none for June after the first two weeks of term. It was the only name he noticed on the list. He managed to stand there while she went on through the book, plodding through German and woodwork, metal-work and keep-fit, and he noted the figures down.

It was all useful research.

Guthrie had taken June to a pub in the country where they had lunch in a timbered bar, knees touching by the low table.

'Terrible about that taxi-driver,' he said. 'Nice young chap he was, too. I met him when some old lady he was driving fainted in your husband's library. I'd meant to book him to drive me to the airport after Christmas. I'm flying to Cyprus to look at some tanks. Now I'll have to find someone else to do it.'

And Audrey had refused to go with him: dug her toes in and said he could do his own research. He'd said it would be a holiday too, and she'd said she'd take hers on her own, thanks very much.

June laid down her fork. In any case she found she had

no appetite for the steak pie confronting her, but here was more proof that Guthrie was a callous man. She thought of how crudely he had propositioned her the other time they lunched together; it had been rather a joke.

Guthrie had not noticed June's *frisson*. He went blithely on.

'That layabout youth must have done it, the one who attacked your Mrs Watson.'

'But he wasn't robbed,' said June. 'Or so the papers said.'

'You mean you believe in this other theory? The jealous husband? There might be something in it – but wouldn't he have waited and attacked the pair of them? Caught them at it?'

Júne could not answer.

'What about a little spin in the car, eh? I'll drop you back in time to fetch the children.'

June looked at his shiny red face and his beard which, streaked with grey, looked scratchy. He was twenty years older than Ted and not a worthy successor, even for later, when Ted's memory had blurred. It did not occur to her to compare him with Cecil.

'I'm afraid I must ask you to take me straight back to the shop,' she said. 'I'm working all day now.'

He patted her knee.

'Never mind,' he said. 'There'll be other occasions.'

The Humber was found that afternoon in the short-stay car park at Luton Airport. It was daubed with Ray Brett's finger-prints. There were other prints in the car too, but not Cecil's. Superintendent Whitchurch, though, still favoured him as a suspect.

'Why not pull him in for questioning?' he demanded, when Purdy said that not a shred of evidence pointed to him. 'Ask him where he was on Wednesday evening for a start.'

'I expect he was at home,' said Purdy. Putting up more

of Notre Dame. 'We're trying to trace who bought that hammer,' he went on. For the one that had struck Ted was new.

Lorna, at the end of the working day, saw Cecil return to The Lindens. As she went past, a police car came towards her. She saw it draw up at the house; Detective Chief Inspector Purdy and another man got out of it, and went up the path to the front door.

Cecil had not even had time to take his coat off when Purdy rang the bell. It was somehow no surprise to see who stood on the step.

'Ah – Inspector Purdy,' he said. 'You want to speak to me?'

'That's right, Mr Titmuss.'

'Would you mind if we talked elsewhere? I don't wish to distress my wife or the children,' said Cecil. 'Could I come down to the station, perhaps?'

'Certainly, if you wish,' said Purdy. Poor bastard: had he done it after all? 'We'll drive you,' he said.

'Very well. I'll just have a word with my wife and then join you, if you'll give me a minute.'

'That's quite all right, Mr Titmuss. Just come out to the car when you're ready,' said Purdy, and stepped back from the door.

He gave the sergeant a nod, and the man went quickly round to the back of the house, in case Cecil meant to make a bolt for it. But Purdy did not think flight was in his mind; the man had a sort of dignity. If he had killed Jessop in a fit of jealous rage, he had the strength to face the consequences.

June and the children were in the kitchen.

'I have to go out, my dear,' he said to June.

'Oh Daddy!' wailed Janet. 'Our chess!'

'I know, pet. We'll play another time,' he promised. He

had just begun to teach her the game. 'I don't expect I'll be long,' he added. 'Barty, you left two of your soldiers out last night and I nearly trod on them. Be more careful when you put them away.'

'Yes, Daddy,' said Barty, abashed.

'June, just a minute, dear,' Cecil said, and to the children, 'I want a word with Mummy.'

June followed him out of the kitchen and into the hall, closing the door.

He knew. Somehow he knew. The police must have told him.

'The police want to see me,' he said in a steady voice, while he watched her.

She had slept with that man, that taxi-driver. It was unbelievable, but it was the truth. However, if he challenged her now the fabric of their marriage would crumble like one of his matchstick buildings if it were crushed.

He had not killed Ted. The inspector was a conscientious man. Somehow, it would all be sorted out in an hour or two and he would come home, free from suspicion. Meanwhile, the marriage, and June, must be protected.

'It's some small matter,' he said. 'Some muddle they think I can help with. A case of mistaken identity. There's nothing to worry about.' He kissed her cheek. 'Don't wait supper if I'm not back, my dear. And lock up after me.'

Lorna saw Cecil leave the house and drive off in the police car.

Had he been arrested? Surely it wasn't possible. She was the only person who knew about June and Ted, and the secret was safe with her. She thought she had safeguarded Cecil for ever, yet now it seemed as if he was in a different sort of peril.

She did not go home, but went instead to the police station, where she loitered in a bus-shelter watching the entrance.

After a while her legs began to ache and she started to shiver, partly because the night was cold but also from nerves. The euphoric sense of power over events which had hitherto buoyed her up had dwindled away, to be replaced by terror. She waited for three hours, but Cecil did not emerge from the police station.

Chapter 25

'I was at home on Wednesday evening. My wife will tell you. I got back at about five-thirty.' Cecil spoke in a steady voice. 'The children were ready for our evening game – we played ludo. Then I read to them. After my wife and I had finished our meal I worked on my model until bedtime. June watched television – it was "Softly, Softly", I remember.' How ironic: a police series. 'She likes that. I am dimly aware of it in the background while I'm working, but I don't pay a lot of attention.'

Purdy believed him. But 'Softly, Softly' was a regular feature, and the attack on Ted had come later than that. He had died somewhere around eleven o'clock, but it was not possible to be absolutely precise about the time.

'Mr Titmuss, do you own a hammer?' asked Purdy.

'Yes. I've two – a large one and a small one,' Cecil said. 'They're in the shed at home.'

'You haven't bought a new one recently?'

Sales of hammers in recent weeks had not been extensive, police enquiries had discovered. Most were cash deals over the counter. Constable Frisby, plodding round the hardware stores, had found this a more agreeable mission than his prowl among the gentlemen's outfitters.

'I put it to you that you discovered your wife was having an affair with Ted Jessop, and you attacked him with intent to kill, some time on Wednesday night,' said Superintendent Whitchurch, taking over the interview.

Cecil, sitting on a hard chair in front of the super-intendent's desk, blenched, but looked at him steadily.

'I did not,' he said.

'You knew Jessop.'

'I met him once, when an old lady he was driving fainted in the library. It was the same old lady who was robbed by that youth, Ray Brett. Surely it was he who attacked Jessop?'

'Jessop was not robbed. Robbery has been the motive for the other attacks in Felsbury,' said Purdy. From where he sat he could see the faces of both the other men: the superintendent, determined to make Titmuss give himself away; the younger man, white and tense, but not afraid.

'You knew your wife was Jessop's mistress?' asked Whitchurch.

'I did not,' Cecil said. He licked his lips; his mouth was quite dry. 'After Inspector Purdy enquired about the Italian tutor I wondered what was in his mind, and why he had come to me. He could more easily have got the answer elsewhere. However, I know now that my wife was not at Italian lessons, as I had supposed, on Tuesday evenings. I have no reason to think she had ever met Jessop.'

'How did you find out your wife had missed the lessons?' asked Purdy.

'I went to the college today, and made an excuse to look at the register.'

Poor devil, thought Purdy.

In the end they gave up. Cecil had no more to add; he knew where Jessop lived because his address was in the papers; he knew what sort of car the man drove, for the papers revealed that too, and anyway he had seen it outside the library. The superintendent went home at last, leaving Purdy with Cecil.

'We'll take you back. I'll fix a car,' said Purdy.

'I didn't do it, you know,' said Cecil.

'I believe you,' Purdy said. 'If we find young Brett quickly we may clear it up without a lot more fuss.'

'I told my wife you wanted to see me about some small matter,' Cecil said. 'If you need to talk to me again, please be good enough to telephone me and I will come round. I don't want her distressed.'

'I hope we won't need to bother you again,' said Purdy. What did he plan to say to his wife when he got home?

'I suppose it's true – about June and Jessop?' said Cecil, showing the first sign of faltering that he had so far displayed.

'I'm afraid it is.'

'How – how did you find out?'

'Jessop had a newspaper cutting – a photograph of her – in his wallet. And we found a scarf of hers.' No need to add more.

'A blue and yellow one? Ah yes – she had lost it.' Cecil nodded. He had given that scarf to June. 'No one knew, then?'

'Oh no. They were very discreet,' said Purdy.

'It will all come out now, though.'

'Not necessarily. Not if we get Brett soon and can prove he did it. He may admit it – we've evidence to link him with the other offences.' Purdy, in his turn, did not wish to be indiscreet, but he felt real pity for Titmuss.

'I always wondered why she married me,' said Cecil.

Purdy had wondered the same thing.

'Some other fellow let her down, just before we met. I was never good enough for her.'

Purdy looked at him, sad, crumpled, near defeat.

'You've got it wrong,' he said roundly. 'She wasn't good enough for you. She's a woman, not a saint – now she's down from that pedestal you'd got her on, you needn't be afraid of her again.'

Cecil stared at him.

'I shall never refer to it,' he said. 'Never.'

208

'But she must realize you've found out.'

'If we bring it into the open there will be a scene. Things may be said that can't be forgotten.' In anger, she might even leave him; with Floradora beckoning, she could be independent. 'We shan't discuss it,' Cecil said. 'Never.'

God, what a punishment for both of them, thought Purdy. I hope we can save you, you poor bugger, he added to himself.

There came a tap at the door and a constable entered.

'Car's here, sir,' he said. 'Round the back, as you said.'

Purdy went with Cecil down the passage to the yard behind the station.

'It's more private this way,' he said. There were reporters at the front.

Lorna, in her refuge, never saw the car leave.

Ray Brett's own face stared back at him, assembled in photofit form from the front of the newspaper held up by the man in the opposite seat.

MAN KILLED IN MEWS ran the headline. From his position across the aisle Ray could not read more. He got off the bus at the next stop, and keeping his head held low, bought a paper from the nearest newsagent's. He took it to a café, bought a cup of tea and sat down to read it. An icy chill came over him as he read about Ted. Who could have done this? It was deliberate murder. His attack on Joyce Watson had not been intended to kill, merely to stun; if he were to be caught for it, it would be manslaughter. But if this one were pinned on him too, he'd be in much worse trouble.

He read on, and learned about the mistress and the theory of the jealous husband. That made sense. He was the one who'd done it, obviously. Maybe they'd find him quickly, and then the hunt would cool down a bit.

He tried to think calmly. The pad in London with the long-legged blonde seemed a distant prospect now.

He must adopt a new identity. His hair, at least, was black now. He'd buy some dye and do it properly. He'd get a suit, too, a business suit. Then he'd find a room in a commercial hotel. He'd grow a moustache, as well; he hadn't shaved since Tuesday, so it shouldn't take long. He might get a job in a shop until things cooled down. He needed respectable surroundings. He'd got no insurance card, though – he would have to say it was lost. There must be some provision for replacements. He would invent a new name for himself.

He felt better when he had made this plan. Birmingham was a huge place with a vast population; when he was absorbed into it no one would find him. He had got there by hitching from Bristol after he'd dumped the car.

After walking around for some time he found a secondhand clothes shop. There were several suits, and he bought one which fitted quite well. He'd look too smart in a new one; it would be conspicuous. He shaved his beard in a public lavatory, leaving the upper lip, then put on his anorak again, but made up his mind to buy a top coat of some sort. He must get a suitcase, too.

It took most of the day to assemble his new *persona*, buying one item in one shop, the others elsewhere, for to get it all at one place would be a mistake. By late afternoon Ray had transformed himself into what the landlady of the commercial hotel to which he applied took to be a meek, well-mannered young clerk. He paid a week's rent in advance and was given an attic room where the waterpipes gurgled behind his bed whenever the cistern emptied. Here, he lifted the threadbare carpet and prised up a floorboard. There was a perfect place for his hoard of wealth.

Then he went out to look for a job.

*

Purdy ran over the facts in his mind after Cecil had gone. He was sure the librarian was innocent of the attack on Ted Jessop. Not a shred of evidence indicated otherwise. Ray Brett's prints were all over the car; a blurred set on the hammer might have belonged to anyone. Whoever carried out the attack doubtless wore gloves, for apart from anything else the night had been cold.

It must have been Brett. Jessop must have surprised him when he was stealing the car. There would be blood on his clothes. Routine enquiries round the cleaners were in progress, but no killer would deposit blood-stained garments openly; Brett would dump them, as he had the holdall he had snatched from Mrs Watson. He'd left nothing in the Humber. Bloodstains in it indicated that Jessop had been attacked while in the car, not on the steps.

If Purdy could not prove it was Brett quickly, the involvement of Cecil Titmuss and his wife in the business would become public knowledge, and then Titmuss would be publicly pilloried. As it was, he was experiencing a private crucifixion.

He'll never be happy again with that beautiful bitch, thought Purdy.

He left his desk at last and went home to his two-roomed bachelor flat, modest but comfortable, in the redeveloped eastern part of the town. He had no woman in his life just now; police hours made it difficult.

He dreamed about June.

Lorna did not sleep that night. There had been nothing about an arrest on the radio news; she had listened every hour. Yet Cecil had not come out of the police station. By the time she had abandoned her vigil she was chilled through, and she was still cold. Twice in the night she got up and made tea. By morning she felt sick and weak. She had eaten nothing since her meagre lunch the day before.

She went out early and bought three papers.

There was no mention of Cecil, but one report said that the police knew the name of the mystery woman involved in the case. From all over England reports were coming in of young men looking like Ray Brett.

'He'll turn up,' thought Lorna. 'They'll find him.'

She turned to the last paper and the line hit her: huge black letters on the back page where some lesser item must have been taken out so that this late news could be printed.

DEPUTY LIBRARIAN HELPS POLICE, said the report, and there was a picture of Cecil and Detective Chief Inspector Purdy entering Felsbury police station together. It was a scoop for the reporter. The text below merely said that they had arrived in a police car; there was nothing to show what subject was interesting them, but the nation knew that Purdy was the inspector investigating Ted Jessop's death.

Lorna bicycled immediately round to the surgery. She let herself in and went up to the office. It was a fine day, very cold, the sort of Saturday Cecil might be in the garden sweeping leaves or having a winter bonfire. She looked out of the window and saw Janet riding her small bicycle round the path that circled the lawn, and Barty hitting a tree in imitation of a woodcutter.

While she watched, June came to the door and called them in. After that, all was quiet. She saw no sign of Cecil.

When Cecil returned from the police station June was in the bath. She had decided, if indeed he did come back, to carry on as normally as possible. It seemed the only thing to do. He had to ring the bell for, obeying his rules, she had put up the chain on the door after he left.

She came down the stairs, damp, wrapped in a towel, her tawny hair pinned up on the top of her head, her face flushed.

'I'm sorry to be so late, dear,' Cecil said calmly. 'Hurry back upstairs or you'll catch cold. I'll just tidy up a few things and then follow. I don't want any supper.' He'd had a cup of tea at the police station.

He waited, staring at nothing, until he knew she must be in bed. In the morning he would be able to face her, but not now; not when she was rosy and warm from her bath and when he found her so desirable. He could not touch her so soon; it would not be decent. Perhaps he never would again.

When he went upstairs at last June seemed to be asleep. He carried out his usual routine, piling his coins tidily on the chest, and undressed in the bathroom, so that he would not disturb her. Finally he slid into bed and wound the clock. He did not kiss her. If he ignored it, the urge in his body might go away; the ache in his heart would remain, he was sure, for ever.

Chapter 26

At seven o'clock on Saturday evening Nancy, Joe and Norman arrived outside the paint shop and rang Lorna's bell. The arrangement was that they would call for her, go for a drink and a meal, and then perhaps visit a discotheque. Lorna had not demurred, but her manner had been vague. However, here they all were, Nancy with a new dress under her fringed sheepskin coat, Joe and Norman with cheerfully patterned shirts and ties showing beneath their warm reefer jackets.

Nancy had warned Norman that Lorna was unlikely to charm him all at once.

'She's all right, when you get to know her,' she said. 'Just a bit stiff.'

Norman was not sure what he had let himself in for. Still, he had no better plans for the evening.

'She must be fixing her false eyelashes,' said Joe, when there was no answer.

Nancy stood back and looked upwards. The windows above the paint shop were dark.

'There's no light up there,' she said.

'Which is her window?' asked Joe.

'I don't know. The top floor, I think.'

'Haven't you been up to her place?' asked Norman.

'No. She's not one for asking you round,' said Nancy.

'Are you sure you fixed to meet her here? Maybe she thought you meant somewhere else,' said Joe.

'No, I said here. I thought that way she wouldn't change her mind.'

'Well, it looks as if she has,' said Norman. 'What shall we do about it?'

'Shove off,' said Joe.

'Let's give her a minute. She may have popped out to the post or something,' said Nancy, unwilling to abandon her kindly scheme.

They waited, getting colder and colder, and ringing the bell at intervals.

'She must have got stage-fright,' Joe said at last. 'Let's leave it.'

After a little more argument from Nancy, who felt that Lorna, though odd and withdrawn, would not run out on a date without saying so, they did.

The telephone was ringing when the Guthries entered their house.

'Who can it be? It's after midnight,' Audrey exclaimed, fearing disaster had struck one of the children.

The Guthries had dined with friends who lived twenty miles away. They had eaten well, drunk plenty, and Peter had boomed away about his new tank series. Already Audrey was heartily sick of Lieutenant Lionel Renshaw, Leo to his cronies, who was destined to rise through the series, book by book, rank by rank, until he became at least a colonel. Perhaps Rommel would get him instead, she had thought hopefully, as she typed one instalment.

'Hullo! Guthrie here,' Peter was saying angrily into the telephone, and added, 'It's probably a wrong number.'

Someone spoke on the line, and he said. 'Don't you realize it's very late? What's all this about?'

The voice persisted.

'You're talking nonsense,' snapped Guthrie and put the receiver down.

'Who was it?' asked Audrey.

'A crank. Some hysterical woman Wanted to talk to you. Lorna something or other. A nut.'

Audrey knew at once who it was.

'Lorna Gibson. Oh, Peter, you shouldn't have cut her off like that.'

After last weekend, she had resolved not to forget the girl but to invite her out again.

'She shouldn't ring up at this hour,' said Guthrie. 'Disturbing people in the middle of the night.'

'She may have been trying to get us all the evening,' said Audrey.

'It can keep till the morning,' said Guthrie, and went upstairs, treading on purposeful feet.

Audrey sighed. He'd had a lot to drink. With luck, if she spun out her undressing and pottered about for a bit, he would be asleep when she got into bed. She felt that she could not endure his heavings and gropings tonight.

She looked in the telephone directory under Gibson. There were a lot of entries, and several with the initial L. She could not call them all at this late hour.

Half an hour later the telephone rang again. Audrey, half smothered, said, 'Answer it, Peter. It must be that girl.'

But he wouldn't. He was past thinking of anyone else but himself.

At six o'clock on Sunday morning, Audrey was in the kitchen drinking tea. You got used to things after years, could shut them out of your mind after a time. Presently, when the boiler had switched itself on and heated the water, she would have a bath. Then she would go to early service, where she need only perform ritual motions with a blank mind; by the time she got back she would feel better. The recipe had worked before.

The telephone rang.

She answered it at once. She'd been so preoccupied with her own humiliation that she had almost forgotten the calls in the small hours of the morning.

'Mrs Guthrie? Oh, thank goodness!'

'Lorna! It is you, Lorna, isn't it?'

'Yes. Oh, Mrs Guthrie, will you help me?'

'Of course I will. What is it?' Audrey said. 'Tell me what's wrong.'

The girl didn't sound hysterical. Her voice was flat emotionless.

'I've been trying to get Inspector Purdy at the police station. In Felsbury. He isn't there. I can't tell anyone else,' Lorna said. Her voice came in a sort of croon.

'Inspector Purdy? What about?'

'Ted Jessop. I killed him. I knew about the Tuesdays,' Lorna said.

'What!' It took Audrey a minute to remember who Ted Jessop was.

'I did it,' Lorna said again.

Peter was right, she was hysterical, though she didn't sound it.

'Where are you speaking from?' Audrey asked.

Lorna ignored the question.

'You were kind to me,' she said. 'There's no one else I can ask. Please will you tell Inspector Purdy that I did it? I bought the hammer at Slater's in Manor Road last Wednesday, and I hid in the back of the car. When Mr Jessop got into it, I hit him. Will you tell Inspector Purdy? It has to be him, no one else will understand.'

She was out of her mind, of course. People did things like this after murders. The police were always getting false confessions.

'Lorna, you need a doctor. Tell me where you are,' said Audrey.

'It doesn't matter. Promise you'll tell Inspector Purdy.

And the Tuesdays. You must remember that. I knew about the Tuesdays.'

'The Tuesdays. Very well. But Lorna –'

'The Tuesdays, remember.'

The phone went dead. Audrey jiggled the receiver. After a minute the dialling tone returned. She hung it up, sat staring at it for some seconds, then lifted it again, to dial 999.

But it wasn't that sort of emergency. It was Felsbury police station that she wanted.

They were very prompt. Audrey convinced them at once that she must speak to Detective Chief Inspector Purdy, and within minutes he rang her back. She repeated her conversation with Lorna as accurately as she could remember it.

'She kept mentioning Tuesday. She said she knew about the Tuesdays,' Audrey said. 'Does that make sense?'

'Oh yes,' Purdy answered. 'Yes, it does.'

Ten minutes after that Purdy, dressed but unshaven, was ringing Lorna's bell.

In the end, they broke the door open, but her room was empty. It was tidy, there was not a thing out of place; Lorna's toothbrush stood in a mug by the sink.

Purdy looked at Constable Frisby, who had met him outside the paint shop.

'Slater's did sell a hammer to a dark-haired woman. That was on your list, wasn't it?' he demanded, and Frisby confirmed that it was.

Purdy looked under Lorna's pillow. The sweater had gone. He searched quickly through her drawers and found the small garments that had belonged to Janet and Barty, which Lorna had put away among her treasures. Beside them, in a polythene bag, was a leatherbound copy of the complete works of Shakespeare. Looking inside, Purdy saw it was inscribed. Lorna had won it as a prize for English Literature at school. There were also some sheets of notepaper bearing sentences composed of letters cut from newspapers. Purdy glanced at them quickly.

'Where can she be?' asked Frisby.

'God knows.'

'She can't have done it,' Frisby said. 'She's a crank. Anonymous letters, yes – but not murder.'

Purdy looked round at the vivid room: Lorna did not lack passion, of a sort.

'We must get after her,' he said.

Several times during the night a woman had rung the station asking for Purdy. She would give no reason, and she sounded calm, so no one had called him. There would be hell to pay about that, later.

Frisby was left to guard the building, while Purdy went back to the station, where he rang Audrey Guthrie, who could throw no more light on the situation.

'She may be wandering around the streets,' said Purdy. 'We've put out a call. Did she ring you from a box?'

'No – no, it wasn't a box. Not this morning, anyway. I don't know about during the night. She rang then, but I didn't talk to her,' Audrey explained. She suddenly realized that while all this was going on, Peter was still asleep. Thank goodness.

'Maybe Mr Vigors could help,' Audrey suggested.

'Vigors?'

'The dentist she worked for. On the corner of Western Grove. He doesn't live there, but that's where his surgery is.'

'Western Grove! Of course, that's it! That's the connection!' The Titmusses lived on the corner where Masterton Road joined Western Grove. 'Where does Vigors live?' Purdy asked. If she knew it would save time.

Audrey did, for she and Peter had been there to dinner.

Ten minutes later the Vigors were woken by peals at the front door bell, and a resentful Bryan, in his dressing-gown, was letting Purdy and his sergeant into the house. The children leaned over the banisters in their pyjamas, watching with interest, until their father sent them back to their rooms with unusual brusqueness.

'What a time to call,' he complained. 'On a Sunday morning. Don't you chaps ever sleep? What is it now? Have I parked where I shouldn't?'

Purdy briefly related the story that Audrey Guthrie had told him.

'Good God, the girl's out of her mind. Of course she couldn't have done it,' Vigors said. 'She's a most un-emotional girl. Hates touching people at all, even old ladies. She'd never attack anyone.'

'She's vanished,' Purdy said. 'She's not in her room – I doubt if she was there at all last night. Have you any idea where she might have gone? Has she any friends?'

'None. Nancy – the other girl who works for me – has tried to make friends with her, I think, but they're not very close. She might be able to help. I can't tell you her home address, I'm afraid. It's round at the surgery, though, on her card in my records.'

'We're going there, then,' said Purdy.

'I suppose I must come and find it for you,' Vigors said with resignation.

'Yes,' said Purdy flatly.

Vigors went upstairs and pulled on a sweater and trousers. His sheepskin coat hung in the cloakroom. All he had time to tell Susan was that that damn girl Lorna had got herself into a rare old scrape this time. Watched goggle-eyed by his children from their window, the dentist was driven off in the police car.

Lorna had done it in the surgery, where the floor was lino-covered. She'd taken time to spread newspaper over the area near the chair. It looked as if she'd tried the gas machine first, for it was beside her, but that hadn't worked; as she lost consciousness her hand had fallen away and the mask had slipped from her face. So she'd cut her radial arteries, and she'd made a good job of it, using one of Vigors' scalpels, and tipping the chair so that she was prone, her arms hanging down, draining on the floor. She was wearing the sweater that Purdy had seen under her pillow, and the receipt for the hammer was propped on the instrument tray in front of her.

She was not quite dead.

Vigors, in this situation as useful as any doctor, acted at once to halt the bleeding, while Purdy called the ambulance. From the office, as he telephoned, he could see Cecil's house, where the day was just beginning. The curtains had been drawn back and the lights were on, for it was a dull morning.

'She'll probably pull round,' said Vigors, when Lorna had been carried off on a stretcher. 'If they can get some blood into her fast enough.' He surveyed the grim scene in his surgery. 'Why did she do it?'

Purdy's mind leaped ahead to the trial that Lorna would have to stand if she did recover: she would not be found unfit to plead, though she might refuse to say a word. The revelation of Cecil's tragedy would become inevitable; there would be no escape

'For love,' he said.

NO MEDALS FOR THE MAJOR

Margaret Yorke

Major Johnson's army career was undistinguished. He rose slowly through the ranks, conforming to the rules, and, on retirement, settled in the quiet village of Wiveldown, where he planned to become a respected member of the community.

But Wiveldown is to belie its placid image, for soon the paths of a disparate group of people are about to cross with devastating consequences. An elderly woman, a pair of young louts, an innocent girl . . . when their lives suddenly connect, a chain of events is initiated which will begin in coincidence and end in tragedy.

And for the Major, life has been irrevocably changed . . .

'Yorke's territory lies behind the net curtains of respectable suburbia . . . No crime writer compares in extracting unease, fear and evil from such placid surfaces'
The Times

FICTION/CRIME
0 7515 1193 5

☐	No Medals for the Major	Margaret Yorke	£4.99
☐	Pieces of Justice	Margaret Yorke	£5.99
☐	Almost the Truth	Margaret Yorke	£4.99

Warner Books now offers an exciting range of quality titles by both established and new authors. All of the books in this series are available from:

Little, Brown and Company (UK),
P.O. Box 11,
Falmouth,
Cornwall TR10 9EN.

Fax No: 01326 317444.
Telephone No: 01326 372400
E-mail: books@barni.avel.co.uk

Payments can be made as follows: cheque, postal order (payable to Little, Brown and Company) or by credit cards, Visa/Access. Do not send cash or currency. UK customers and B.F.P.O. please allow £1.00 for postage and packing for the first book, plus 50p for the second book, plus 30p for each additional book up to a maximum charge of £3.00 (7 books plus).

Overseas customers including Ireland, please allow £2.00 for the first book plus £1.00 for the second book, plus 50p for each additional book.

NAME (Block Letters) ....

....

ADDRESS ....

....

....

☐ I enclose my remittance for ....

☐ I wish to pay by Access/Visa Card

Number ⬚⬚⬚⬚⬚⬚⬚⬚⬚⬚⬚⬚⬚⬚⬚⬚

Card Expiry Date ⬚⬚⬚⬚